The Beat on Ruby's Street

Jenna Zark

DMP

PRINT ISBN 978-1-988256-18-4

EPUB ISBN 978-1-988256-19-1

Library of Congress Control Number: 2015954131

Printed on acid free paper

Cover Design by Gwen Gades

Edited by Andie Gibson

www.dragonmoonpress.com

To Pete, Josh, Max, and Faye for letting the light in;
To the poets, wherever you are, for inspiration and the seed

Contents

Acknowledgments

This book is dedicated to Susan Jeffers Casel, whose encouragement and insight were matched only by her careful attention to detail during the early phases of this book. In addition, I am grateful to Book Manager Pamela Labbe for her encouragement, exquisite graphics, wit and wisdom. Thanks are also due to Vay David, who lived under the gypsy fortune-teller's shop on Bedford Street in Greenwich Village; sister Lesley, niece Tara, and her dad, Ernie, who lived on Perry Street; neighbors for sharing stories of Village life in the fifties; and Jorie Latham, Mara Miller, Sean Murphy and Janet Stilson for their insights on earlier drafts.

1
At the Station

THERE'S A GUY in the neighborhood who wrote a book on toilet paper. They made it into a real book, but when he first wrote it you could unwind it all the way uptown and back again.

His name is Jack Kerouac and I was on my way to see him at The Scene, when I got waylaid by a blood orange. Now I'm in the police station, and my mother's going to eat me alive. She hates police and social workers, and I'm knee deep in both of them. When my mom was a kid a social worker came by because my grandmother had a car accident and wasn't like she used to be. So the kids ended up with foster parents and only saw their own parents on holidays. That's what social workers do.

The one sitting next to me seems like she's trying to be nice at least. She brought some ice for my arm, which got pretty twisted up after Tattoo Tina grabbed it.

I was trying to put the apples back on her fruit stand because they were falling. Where I live in Greenwich Village, they have all these bins on the sidewalk in front of stores. The bins are piled high with fruits and stuff, and yes, I was trying to move an apple out of the section next to the blood oranges. I love blood oranges—in fact, they're my favorite—but these were kind of wet and the apple was getting sticky. So I was trying to do a good deed.

Of course, Tattoo Tina would disagree. She's not much taller than me but her arms are a lot thicker, with ripply muscles like ropes and tattoos on top of them. As soon as I touched the oranges she reached her hand out and grabbed my wrist.

"Watcha doin', little robber girl?"

I wanted to say "Who you calling a little robber girl?" and leave it at that. But she was grabbing me so tightly I got mad and put my foot down as hard as I could—on hers.

I don't think it hurt too much because she wears these hard leather boots, but just the idea of me—or anyone—defying her makes Tina purple with rage. The next thing I know, she's screaming, "Okay! You want to play rough?" which sounded like "woof" because she was mad. That started me laughing and then like clockwork, she's twisting my arm.

So now, okay. I should have stopped at this point, gone limp or something until she calmed down. But I've seen Tina drive my best friend Sophie to tears, and once she pushed my friend Gordy so hard he almost lost a tooth. That happened when Sophie dropped her money in the store and got down on all fours to find it. Sophie can't do much of anything without making a joke, so she pretended to be a dog, sniffing around the floor for money. She had Gordy and me laughing so hard we nearly fell over, and Tina came out from behind the counter.

All of a sudden she was screaming bloody murder, which scared Sophie so bad she started to shake, and then Gordy got protective, standing in front of us and telling Tina to cool it. Instead, she shoved him and called him a dummy, which is pretty funny considering how many numbers Gordy can add in his head.

So even though it was crazy, I was not about to knuckle under. I swung my other arm to make all the apples and blood oranges roll off the shelves. By this time Tina was howling and I thought if I kicked her, she'd let go. Instead she twisted my arm even harder—so hard it took my breath away.

Then Tina yelled, "Thief!" The cop outside rushed in and everyone looked at me like I was a cockroach, which I felt like, pretty much. Now I'm in the Greenwich Village police station with a social worker, a slew of policemen tramping in and out with people they've arrested, a bum trying to sleep on a bench by the door, and worst of all, no hope of seeing Jack Kerouac.

That makes me sadder and madder than getting my arm twisted because I've been making up poems since I was four, even though I didn't start writing until I was seven. I want to read at The Scene one day but you have to be old enough. Plus, mostly famous like Kerouac who isn't a poet, really, but writes like one. And the only way you get to be good at writing is by listening to other people. I think you really need to hear them because poetry is about rhythm as much as anything.

I waited a month to see Kerouac and now I'm stuck in this station with questions coming from all directions. But if I tell the truth I'll open a big, smelly can of worms. I try to keep mum, which doesn't work very well because the questions keep coming. Then I get an idea. I can tell the truth in a kinda-sorta way, like salesmen do when they want you to buy something. "Name?"

"Ruby Tabeata." Our name used to be Tabita, but my dad changed it when I was small. For the Beat, which is a secret way of saying we're part of the Beat Generation. When it started, it was about people who were fed up and beat up by the System. That means the world, really—or most of the world.

The magazines call us "Beatniks," which makes us laugh because it sounds so stupid. What I think is, people are mostly asleep and when they come down here to see guys like Jack Kerouac, it's because they're hungry for something and Jack fills them up. They want to hear about him driving around the country, meeting people, and seeing things they'll never see. They want to listen to poets like Allen Ginsberg who says the best minds of his generation are getting stomped on by the world.

Ginsberg found a place in the Village and started writing poetry, and pretty soon other cats came down and started writing, too. Now a lot of artists live in this neighborhood, which is below Fourteenth Street but not as far as Houston.

I guess you could say we're trying to break out of the old world and start a new one. But that's not something you can explain to a social worker or policeman. They think the old world is just fine.

The magazines also say Beats are supposed to be cool, but who knows what that means? I can only tell you what it's not. It's not cool to be angry or nasty. It's not cool to care about how you look. Because like my mother says, pretty fades, but cool is forever. And having a name like Tabeata says all that. But the phone book still says Tabita because it was never officially changed.

"Date of birth?" the policeman asks.

I toy with making something up but decide on the truth. "April 12, 1946."

"You're going to be twelve soon?"

It's my golden birthday, but I don't say much about that. Because I'm turning twelve on April 12 and it's supposed to be super-extra lucky. If I mention it now I'll jinx it for sure.

"Address?"

"Ninety-six Bleecker," I say, even though it's *really* 96 Perry.

They want to know my parents' names.

I call my father "Gary Daddy-o." It's kind of a joke we have, because all the Beat guys call each other "Daddy-o" when they're goofing on how Beats talk in the movies. I tell the policeman his name is Gerard, which is my dad's given name even though he never uses it. He's like one of those cats you see on bongos, except he doesn't play bongos, he plays bass.

My mother's name is Nell and we call her "Little Nell" because she's the tallest one in her family. I mostly call her Nell-mom, which she likes better than plain old Mom. Too old and too old-fashioned, she says. She has long, curly hair from Wisconsin and the rest of her is from Wisconsin, too. Little Nell does oils and etchings, all different kinds. Sometimes she does abstracts, which are all these shapes and colors. Other times it's ladies and they're not wearing very much. It's not sexy, she says. It's sophisticated.

Nell-mom paints at a studio near Christopher Street on Saturdays and she's there right now but I'm not going to tell anyone. The last thing in the world you want to do is interrupt Nell-mom when she's at the studio. She needs *TIME TIME TIME* to paint and if she doesn't get that, we hear about it. Over and over again.

I have an older brother, Ray, who is fourteen and never, ever gets in trouble. It's not that he doesn't do anything wrong. He just knows how to get away with it. Ray's one of those quiet guys who fades into the background unless he's playing saxophone. Then you want to stop what you're doing and listen; that's how he gets the girls coming around.

They say Ray's pretty dreamy, and I guess he is, with Nell-mom's curly brown hair and blue eyes. But you don't think that way when someone's your brother. I could tell you more about his leaving every piece of clothing he owns all over the house than what he looks like—and forget about food when he's around because he scarfs up everything in sight.

I'm guessing Ray's with Les and Bo today. They're studio musicians who play on record albums. They also give music lessons, and Ray is one of their students. He usually goes over there Saturdays to play with a bunch of people in what they call a jam. Gary Daddy-o could be there, too, unless he's juggling.

Gary Daddy-o goes out on the road a lot to play at clubs, either upstate or in Boston or Philadelphia. When he's here he puts a cup down in the subway and juggles oranges, and if Ray tags along and plays saxophone, they almost always draw a crowd. If enough people put money in Gary Daddy-o's cup, we get steak for dinner. Nell-mom has a job at an art store and gets free supplies, which she likes. But they both wish they could just play music and paint.

They're kinda-sorta married, in a kinda-sorta way. They've been together a long time so it seems like they're married, even though they don't have a marriage license. That's how a lot of people are down here. Gary Daddy-o says 1958 will be a good year because there was a big article about the Beats in *Life* magazine and a lot of tourists are coming. That means a lot of people will be in the subways, which means more money can find its way into his cup.

"Where are your parents today?" the social worker asks. Her name is Mrs. Levitt and she's got short blond hair and stockings. The cops call her "Levitt," like she's a man.

"I'm not sure about my dad. My mom is either painting or at work."

"Okay," she says. "Shall we go find her?"

"What if we can't?"

She sighs. "Then we'll have to come back here."

I get the feeling she doesn't want to do that, and I don't either. But finding Little Nell will be worse. I'm trying to decide what to do as we move toward the door. When I pass the bench I realize the guy sleeping on it is someone I know.

He sits under the arch most days at Washington Square Park with his legs curved underneath him like a pretzel. He went to India and says that's what yogis do, so that's what we call him.

"Yogi?"

He opens one eye and looks at me.

"Hey, kid. What are you in for?"

I tell him about the blood orange touching the apple and how it was all Tina's fault when he interrupts me.

"That's your problem right there," he says.

"What do you mean?"

"Mixin' apples and oranges. She had it all balanced, didn't she?"

"Who, Tina?"

"She had it right and you tipped the apple cart. Literally."

"Yogi—"

"Everything is there for a reason, right? If you mess with it like that, you're not following the flow of the universe. It's like trying to float upstream."

I try not to sigh, because once Yogi gets going there's no stopping him, and I'm not sure, even if I do explain, that he really wants to understand. "Okay, well, right," I say. "What are you in for?"

"Being," Yogi says. "Being and nothingness."

He always says things like that. He calls them Zen sayings. You can't argue with them because they don't make sense in the first place. So you just have to smile and let it go.

"Ruby?"

Mrs. Levitt is calling me.

"I hope you get out of here soon, Yogi," I tell him.

"Okay, Ruby," says Levitt. "Let's go."

I poke my head out the door, looking up and down the street. I'm hoping Sophie and Gordy will be off somewhere, preferably together so I won't run into them. There's not that many kids my age in the Village besides them and Ray, but he's so tall you might not know he's a kid. He has a girlfriend but she goes to a regular school, so she doesn't have much to worry about.

Sophie, me, Ray, and Gordy, on the other hand, are a different story. We're supposed to be at P.S. 41, which is a normal-looking school on West Eleventh. But, like I said, people here are trying to throw out the old rules. So Nell-mom and Gary Daddy-o thought we should go to a school that would teach us more about how to live and less about pleasing a teacher. Sophie's mom, Mrs. Tania, and Gordy's parents agreed.

Now here's what I mean when I talk about a can of worms. There's a store in the Village called Blue Skies that's owned by a couple named Sky and Blu. Sky is short for Skylar, Blu for Bluma, and they just figured they belonged together. Because Sky used to be an English teacher, he said he would teach us if we helped out behind the register—and pay us, too. So Nell-mom, Mrs. Tania, and Gordy's dad fixed the place up and take turns cleaning it. And that's where we go to school.

Blue Skies is kind of a candy store but has all kinds of other stuff, too—posters, magazines, stuff for motorcycles. Classes start at all different times—like whenever we feel like it, and we make up our own homework. We read poetry and learn math by running the cash register. Gordy's really good at numbers, so he shows us how to do times tables and long division. If you count lunch and recess, it's almost like a regular school.

But it's not really allowed and we're not supposed to talk about it. And if I hadn't got in trouble with Tattoo Tina, I wouldn't have to. I can still keep it a secret, but I'm going to have to be careful. Once Mrs. Levitt gets ahold of this I don't know what she'll do.

"Ready?" She holds the door open for me.

I skip outside like I haven't got a care in the world. But once I'm outside the station house I go down the stairs slowly, blocking Mrs. Levitt's way so she has to follow me. If I time it right, I can get into the alley before she sees me. Then I can run.

2
Underground

MACDOUGAL ALLEY is full of tourists and street musicians. Normally I'd stop in front of the pet store to see the kittens but all I'm looking for now is an escape.

"Where are we going, Ruby?" Mrs. Levitt asks.

"I thought we'd try the art store. My mom works there."

"Is she there today?"

"I think so. She's there every other Saturday."

Levitt gets quiet, letting me lead the way. The smell of bread comes out of Smoky's and it's all I can do not to run in there. I haven't eaten since breakfast and it's already one o'clock.

I stop and look up at Levitt, shading my eyes. "Would you—could I have something to eat, please?"

"You mean you're hungry?"

"Well, uh, sure."

She buys me a roast beef sandwich and an orange juice. I ask for a Coke but she wants me to have milk, so we compromise.

"Have you eaten today, Ruby?" she asks.

"Oh, sure," I say.

"What did you have?"

She's asking to build a case against me. Or Nell-mom and Gary Daddy-o. If she can prove my parents aren't taking care of me, she can become my caseworker. Then she can get money—which, by the way, doesn't go to my family. It just makes it easier for someone like Levitt to stick her nose in my life.

"Pancakes," I say, yawning, which is a good thing to do when you're making stuff up. For some reason people tend to believe what you're saying more if you yawn. My real breakfast was cereal but I think pancakes sounds homier—like something you'd have if you lived in Queens, which is a borough east of Manhattan. New York has five boroughs, and Queens has most of the normal, homey, pancake-eaters. I think.

"Where's the art store?" Levitt asks, and I slide off the stool and say I'll show her. We're at the cash register when I look across the street and see exactly what I've been looking for.

The cellar door below Sorocco's Wines is open, next to the gypsy fortune-teller's. Most people stay away from gypsies but I like to wave when I pass them and they always wave back to me. Nell-mom says it's because I look like them, with dark eyes and hair going loose down my back. They wear big, hoopy earrings that I'd do anything for but they cost at least ten dollars. I kid you not.

The lady behind the cash register is counting out Levitt's change and I realize it's now or never. I scoot out the door, jumping into the crowd before she can even turn around. As I rush down into the cellar I hear her yelling from across the street.

"Ruby! Hey!"

Five, six, seven steps, and another door. I open it and run down more steps to a musty-smelling tunnel. It's dark, cold, and wet and I have to keep my hand on the wall to feel my way.

I'm inching forward in baby steps when I see a light that seems to be coming from underneath another door. I have no idea where I am at this point because cellars in the city go on forever. The cellar under Sophie's apartment goes all the way to Chinatown, which is like ten city blocks and has only Chinese people. I know because we followed it once and wound up under a bakery that sold thousand-year-old eggs. This tunnel seems like it's still under the wine store but I can't be sure.

I reach down and put my hand on a knob that opens easily, and all of a sudden I'm in a kind of storage closet lined with wine bottles. At least I can see in here.

I walk inside, looking at the shelves that stretch from floor to ceiling. They have pink wines on one side and white on the other. On the far side of the wall are burgundy reds. Nell-mom and Gary Daddy-o like those, so we always have some at home.

I'm staring at a row of them when the door behind me shuts and I hear a clicking sound. My heart starts beating very fast because I know what that means. The door slipped and if no one's around to hear it, I'm going to be here for a while.

I should tell you I'm claustrophobic, meaning scared of small spaces, like closets and elevators. I know it's dumb but I've been that way since I was little and I've never been able to shake it no matter what I do. It's always felt like if I'm in a place with no way out, the walls are closing in on me. And that's exactly what I feel like now. I turn the knob and sure enough, it's locked. I jiggle and pull on it but it's not budging and I can feel sweat on the back of my neck. I start breathing slowly, which is what they always tell you to do when you're panicking. I try the door again but it's tight as a drum.

The closet floor is carpeted and I sit down, trying to think. Someone's got to show up at some point to get wine. Of course it could take days and there's no window in here. I heard there was a kid once who suffocated in a closet when he ran out of air.

Beat heat — street fleet.

I've been working on this poem and for some reason, the words start running through my head.

Beat heat—street fleet.

Sky says you have to trust your poetry. You can set it up in your mind but without trust, it won't unfold. It will sound like you're trying to con someone into thinking it's poetry—but it won't be real.

> *Sweet fleet beat of the street*
> *Rising heat*
> *From the white of the sidewalk*
> *And the conga sound of the*
> *Bonga bonga bongos*
> *BEAT. BEAT. BEAT.*

My heart is going crazy. I close my eyes and say the words:

> *"Every spring*
> *They sprout like toadstools*
> *In the key of heat"*

I take out my notebook and pen to start writing, propping it up on my knees. Nell-mom bought it for me more than a year ago. It's green leather and used to have a key, but I lost it somewhere. She bought it at the art store and totally embarrassed me by saying I would be an amazing poet if she could just get me to write stuff down. But then someone said not a lot of moms would even read their kid's poetry, let alone buy them a notebook for it. So that made me feel better.

I open the notebook and scribble the first verse but the carpet is hard and prickly and I could swear something's dripping in here. It could be wine, which means it will be sweet and sticky. And that means bugs.

A centipede skitters across the wall behind the wine shelves. We have them in the bathroom at home sometimes, but our cat chases them. Her name is Solange and she's black all over. She eats remnants, which is another word for scraps. I think she needs company but Nell-mom says we barely have enough to feed Ray and me, let alone a cat. So I don't think we'll get another one any time soon.

There's a tiny little snuffling sound behind me and I'm pretty sure I know what that is, too. We had mice before Solange came and you could hear them skittering in the hall at night. Sometimes we still find one—or half of one—but Solange scared most of them off, so I think they're skittering in someone else's place. They could really use a cat in here, too.

I jump up and start kicking at the door even though I know it won't do any good. I start yelling, too; I can't help it. Then I stop.

Yelling makes you panic even more and I want to stop panicking. The room seems a teeny bit smaller than when I came in, but I know it's my imagination. I KNOW it. Gary Daddy-o says he also gets the hee-bie-jeebies about being stuck in small spaces. That's why he never goes into an elevator unless there's at least one other person in there.

I jiggle the doorknob again, trying to see if I can trip the lock. Nothing budges so I kick at the door a few more times, but no one's coming. I am not. Not. Not going to be a crybaby. That is totally uncool—it is the opposite of cool.

I lean against the door trying to think of all the things I can name that are also the opposite of cool—mostly to keep myself from crying. I would probably start with school and school uniforms. Murray Hill and Park Avenue where the rich people live. Suburbs like Rye and White Plains. Anything pink that has ruffles or ribbons. Anything in New Jersey—except for the George Washington Bridge.

I first saw it from a car window when a friend of Gary Daddy-o's drove us home from a party New Year's Eve. The night I saw it, someone said the lights made it look like a pearl necklace, which I wrote down in my notebook. If you want to be any kind of writer, you should always have a notebook with you.

Beat heat—street fleet.

I hear that snuffling again from somewhere above me. I look up and see it—a tiny gray mouse on top of a wine bottle. If it's wine he's after, he's going to have plenty of it. Maybe it will make him drunk and he'll go to sleep.

Gordy once said if you're ever in trouble, scream "Fire!" because more people will rush over to help you. But if people come and there is no fire, they might get mad and say you don't deserve their help. On the other hand, I'm starting to panic again and decide I have nothing to lose.

"FIRE! FIRE!!! HELP!"

I throw myself at the door a few times, but all that happens is it shakes a little bit. The only one who seems to notice anything at all is the mouse, who looks down at me for a second and then disappears. Nothing else makes a sound.

If I ever do get out of here I'm never going anywhere near that stupid fruit store. I'm never going back to MacDougal Alley. And I am for sure never going anywhere near an open cellar for the rest of my stupid life.

I look around to see if there's something I can throw at the ceiling, but all I see are bottles, wall to wall. I really don't want to break one unless I have to.

"Somebody HELP—"

I kick and pound the door as hard as I can.

"Who is that? Who's there?"

A man's voice calls from somewhere in the hallway—and my heart starts pounding again. I want to get out of here more than anything but that guy could be anyone. The city's full of perverts and they all live in cellars—everybody knows that.

The doorknob rattles just as the snuffling starts up again. The knob is turning and I step back against the wall. I look up at the row of wine bottles and put my hand on them. If he jumps me I can break a bottle over his head like they do in movies and maybe scare him off.

He doesn't seem to have a key because I hear banging like he's trying to break down the door. That makes me think he really *is* a pervert so I grab a bottle and pull it off the shelf—which turns out to be a big mistake. Now all the bottles are shaking.

I must have knocked them pretty good because the ones on the top shelf are tipping over. I don't think I can look anymore. I close my eyes just as the door opens, and a whole row of bottles comes hurtling down at my head.

3
House of Sorocco's

A WIRY-LOOKING MAN with dark hair and bony shoulders sticking out of his undershirt opens the door. The girl standing next to him looks about seventeen, but it's too dark to tell if she's someone I know.

"Sorry, I got . . . stuck," I say, gesturing lamely at the floor. Luckily, only three bottles fell and only one of them broke, but the man is acting like I broke all of them.

"What are you DOING in here?" he shouts, and I'm so relieved to be out of there I almost start crying.

"Someone was chasing me," I say, "so I ran in here. Then the door locked and when you opened it, all the bottles fell."

"Elena." He gestures to the girl and then turns to look at her. "Don't let her step on the glass."

His voice is starting to sound familiar and I'm trying to figure out where I heard it when Elena steps forward. I recognize her right away. She works at Sorocco's Restaurant on Bleecker, dishing out lasagna, cannoli, and Italian ices. I doubt she knows me because Sorocco's is always crowded and I only go when I have money, which isn't much because I'm saving for a leotard.

If the man with the undershirt is Elena's father, then I'm guessing he's Mr. Sorocco and owns both the restaurant and wine store. Elena usually works with her mom, who has an Italian accent and a stern-looking face with a long nose and chin. Most people try to get Elena to serve them. She has long, dark hair and lips like Sophia Loren.

Elena kneels to pick up some of the glass and I lean down to help her. She's wearing a wine-red leotard and smells like Fabergé, which is my favorite perfume. Elena is secretly engaged to Jimmy from Buka's Bakery. Even though everyone in the neighborhood knows, her parents don't have a clue. She has to wait until she's eighteen to marry Jimmy anyway, but her mom doesn't like him and shoos him off every chance she gets.

Elena puts most of the glass in a pile, and I start picking up splinters. She puts her hand over mine and says, "No." I look up and she says, "My father's getting a vacuum." I nod and pick up one of the other bottles, setting it against the wall so it won't break. Meanwhile Elena is staring at the wine stain on the carpet. "I didn't mean to spill anything," I say, but I don't think she's listening. Instead, she touches the stain and says, "Horse."

"What?"

"The spill makes a horse shape," she tells me. "See?" Elena starts tracing the shape but I can't see anything. "I can't figure out if he has a saddle or just a mane."

"What does that mean?"

"Well, the gypsies say if it has a saddle that means you're going to marry someone poor."

"What if it's a mane?"

"Then your husband will be rich and famous."

"Really?" I stare at the wine stain, trying to figure out if it has a saddle or not. But Jimmy isn't rich so if she wants that, why is she engaged to him?

"Did you ever get your fortune told?" I ask.

Instead of answering, Elena gets up to help her father, who is dragging the vacuum cleaner downstairs. When he turns it on you can hear little slivers of glass shooting inside it, which make a crackling sound. He runs it up and down the length of the closet until all the glass is gone. As soon as he shuts it off, I look up at him sad-eyed, hoping I can get out of there.

"I gotta go—"

"Come with me," he says, and turns around without another word. I could try and leave the way I came but I'm kind of turned around and don't want to end up in another cellar. Elena leans toward me and whispers, "Don't worry. His bark is worse than his bite." She touches my arm lightly and leads me up the stairs behind her dad.

We go through a painted wooden door into a room that smells like sausages. A large kitchen table is full of pots, and the pots are full of soup and tomatoes. There's a freezer the size of a small room, and I think someone's elbow is poking out of it. Elena calls out, "Ma!" but no one appears. Then I realize the person in the freezer is Mrs. Sorocco. "She'll be out soon," Elena tells me. "She goes in when it's hot."

It doesn't seem very hot to me, but when Mrs. Sorocco comes out it seems like she could have stayed in the freezer much longer. The hairs on her upper lip are wet, and her cheeks are flushed and dripping. She tugs at the neck of her sweater, which has raggedy armholes where she cut off the sleeves.

"This the child?" she asks, but no one answers, and the line between her eyes darkens as she frowns. "How many break, Angelo?"

The man with the undershirt holds up his finger.

"Zo," Mrs. Sorocco says, turning to me. "You are going pay?"

"Sure," I say, "but I don't have a lot of money right now."

"How much you got?"

"Two bucks," I tell her.

"Not enough," Mrs. Sorocco says. "A bottle is ten dollar."

"I'm sorry," I say, trying to look shaken.

"Sorry don't fix it," she says, closing the freezer door and folding her arms.

"I know," I say. "But what can I do?"

"Either pay," Mrs. Sorocco says, "or work," only she pronounces it "vark."

I'm feeling around in my pocket for a five-dollar bill. I've been desperate for a leotard the past year and a half, and today was the day I was going to get one, right after Kerouac. The leotard store is on the corner of West Tenth and is owned by a woman named Cyn, who says if I put five dollars down she'll hold one, and I know just the one I want. It's bright red, not wine colored like Elena's, and Cyn says I'd look great in it. She ought to know because she studies at the Fashion Institute uptown.

Cyn wears black eyeliner and glasses with little tails on the ends. She doesn't talk to customers unless she knows them. Even then she's not big on talking much. If you want to try on a leotard she motions with her head to the fitting room, which is behind a red velvet curtain in back of the store. Meanwhile she sits mostly on a stool smoking Lucky Strikes. She also wears hoopy earrings. I've had my eye on a pair just like them in the store, but don't even have close to the ten bucks they'll cost me. I've been running the cash register at Blue Skies forever, and it will take at least six months to save up another five dollars and I can't give up my pay no matter what happens. I really, truly can't.

"You vark in store with us?" Mrs. Sorocco asks.

"Mama," says Elena, "she doesn't know how to work in a store."

"Anyone can," says Mrs. Sorocco. "She sweep and clean up after school, yes? Maybe two days a week."

"I don't have time," I say.

"Vark or pay, miss," says Mrs. Sorocco. "You not get away without paying."

"What if I don't?" I say.

"We call police," Mr. Sorocco says.

Why is everyone calling the cops on me today?

"Look," I say to Mrs. Sorocco. "I'm supposed to work at another store. If I work at this one I won't even get paid—"

"For three weeks, maybe month," she tells me. "Then you are done with us."

Great. So not only do I not make money for a leotard, I don't make any money at all because I broke something by accident. Why did I get up today?

Mrs. Sorocco leans closer to me. "Vaht your name is?"

"Ruby," I say glumly. "But that wine isn't worth ten dollars—"

"HEY—" Mr. Sorocco yells, but his wife holds out her arm.

"Angelo—"

"It's not even worth two dollars!"

"She's a fresh kid—" he says.

"Daddy!" Elena calls out. "Leave her alone."

He glares at me for a minute or two and turns away, and Mrs. Sorocco picks up her knife and starts smashing garlic.

"Elena," she says. "Take her out."

"Yes, Mama."

"Look," I tell her. "I have to ask my mother—"

"Ze good," she says. "We tell her you break bottle—"

"No, wait—" I say, but we both know she has me. I let out my breath and look at the floor. "All right already."

"Could start on Monday," Mrs. Sorocco says. "In afternoon."

"I can't work Monday," I say. "Wednesday or Saturday."

"Both," she answers. "You come Wednesday at half past three."

Well. At least I can still put money down on my leotard. So I guess I shouldn't complain.

"You go now?" says Mrs. Sorocco.

"Yeah." I look up at Elena. "Where do I go?"

Mr. Sorocco looks at his daughter. "Elena will show you."

I follow her out of the kitchen and down the stairs, but instead of turning to go out the front by the wine store, Elena takes me to a door at the end of the hall.

"It's not all bad," Elena says. "You get a free cookie at the end of your shift." I try to smile so as not to hurt her feelings. I like cookies as much as anyone but the cookies in that store are tiny. And they can't make up for sweeping and cleaning. Ever.

I step outside and Elena closes the door. It's really bright compared to the shop and I put my hand up to shade my eyes. I'm in back of MacDougal Alley but since I never come this way, I'm still kind of turned around. I trudge forward a little and then start running, glad to be out of there. I'm almost to the end of the alley when I realize I better slow down. I lean out a bit to peer up the street.

A couple is getting out of a Checker cab on the corner. Those are my favorite kind because of the Checker pattern on the sides. The couple is having an argument, and the woman slaps the man and walks off. A second or two later, her shoe breaks, only instead of putting it back on, she takes them both off and throws them at him. He ducks and gets back inside the cab and then it speeds away.

I stand there a minute, watching. Little Nell would never slap Gary Daddy-o and I've only seen ladies do stuff like that in the movies. There's something about it, though, that makes you think. What would it be like to haul off and slap your man?

All of a sudden she looks right at me and I have to start walking again. I pass a basketball court and a group of boys shooting baskets. Across the street is what looks to be a long line of people waiting to get into the movies. I'm at West Fourth and Sixth, about a half block from Waverly. I edge forward as slowly as I can, trying to snake my way to the corner when someone calls out my name.

"Ruby!"

I don't have to look up to know it's Sophie. I put my finger up to my mouth.

"Shhhh!"

Sophie runs over, peering at me like I'm from Outer Mongolia. "What's the matter? What's wrong?"

How do you tell your best friend you're running away from the police? Especially when she's the worst person on the planet when it comes to keeping secrets?

"Ruby?" Sophie says again.

I pull her into the alley, and her blue eyes go wide.

Here we go.

4
Kerouac Dreams

SOPHIE PUSHES her glasses up so they're resting on her head and squints at me. "What's eating you?"

"Nothing," I say, and start walking.

"Weren't you going to the reading today?"

"Yeah," I tell her. "I got tied up."

"Not literally," she says, smiling.

"Not literally," I repeat.

"Ruby," Sophie says. "WHAT is going on?"

We edge around the basketball court and into another alley after crossing over Waverly. "I got . . . stuck at Tina's," I say finally.

"Oh," Sophie answers, and I let her ponder that for a while. "You okay?"

"I think so. Was he good?"

"You mean Kerouac?" she says.

"Who else?"

"Truth?" Sophie pulls her glasses down and looks at me. "I was late because of the lunch thing. I couldn't even get in."

Sophie's mom is a comic and writes television scenes and sketches at the Fisk Building. Every other weekend the writers get together for lunch and this week they were at Sophie's. And since she wants to be an actress she would naturally like being around a bunch of TV writers. But still.

"It was Kerouac."

"Well, you skipped it, too, Ruby."

I scowled. "I didn't mean to skip it. That was Tina's fault."

"Did she hit you?"

"She twisted my arm."

"You're *kidding*! That's *terrible*!"

"Shhh!" I put my hand to my mouth. The last thing I need is to get people watching us.

"What's the matter with you today?"

"Nothing," I sigh. One of these days Sophie's going to have a secret and want *me* to keep it and then the tables will be turned.

Don't get me wrong—Sophie can be more fun than anyone else I know. Her mom taught her all these jokes and she does them with character voices, imitating stars like Eve Arden and Imogene Coca. Put Sophie next to Gordy, who collects facts like candy because his main ambition is to win a quiz show contest—and the two of them are a blast.

Once, the three of us got on the D train at West Fourth and it was truly a creature car. Sophie twisted up her shoulder like the Hunchback of Notre Dame and we laughed so hard our faces hurt. Then Gordy recited the names of every nut in the world—filberts, almonds, walnuts, you name it—and Sophie pretended she was eating them. My favorite thing is, whenever it starts to go quiet, Sophie will do something outrageous—like tossing her head and saying, "Oh, mercy!" in a Donald Duck voice. And all of a sudden we're cracking up again.

But I know right now, today, if I say anything about what happened Sophie will go crazy, and the last thing I need is people staring at us while my friend jumps up and down like a maniac. So I just keep walking and hoping for the best.

We get to the end of the alley and turn left, heading over to West Tenth. If I can still get my leotard, the day won't be a total loss. We pass The Coat of Many Colors, where Nell-mom works, though not on weekends anymore.

It's about as perfect looking a day as you'll ever see in the Village, with sunlight pouring down on brownstones, and guitar music floating out of windows. We pass a man on stilts and a group of guys singing doo-wop harmonies. The guy in the middle is really belting it out and even smiles at me. If his hair were a little shorter, he'd look almost like James Dean.

I wave at him and Sophie bumps me, grinning. She's always accusing me of having crushes on guys I barely know even though she's much worse than I am. I bump her back and we giggle. I'm starting to get in a better mood and think about going by The Scene after the leotard store. Of course the reading will be over, but there might be something—say, something Kerouac left behind. A pen, maybe, or a scrap of paper. That happens a lot of times when people have readings. Sophie found a quarter she swears fell out of Ginsberg's wallet, so why couldn't I find something of Jack's?

What would happen if I found it? Would I keep it or give it back? If it was a pen I'd maybe keep it but if it was a piece of paper—say, with his writing—I'd have to give it back, even if it meant asking everyone I knew. They would all say, "Hey, Ruby," when they saw me coming, knowing I had this piece of writing by Jack Kerouac and was trying to find him.

Eventually he'd hear about it and maybe he would have forgotten he'd lost it and written a whole different set of words. Then when I found him he'd realize, no, that was the sentence he was looking for, just a fragment maybe, but a really important fragment that changed the entire story he wrote. When he saw it, he'd look at me with those big, dark eyes and for a minute, the two of us would stand there, not saying anything.

I'd pull the piece of paper out of my book bag, which is where I'd be keeping it, and maybe look down at his boots, all muddy and scruffy. He'd lift my chin so I'd look at him and I'd hand him the paper or, no, just hold it up in front of him so he could see the words. And he'd fall at my feet like Marlon Brando does in *A Streetcar Named Desire*, and if it wasn't too corny I'd put my hand on his head, and we'd both just stay there, me and Kerouac, in the middle of the street with everyone else looking on.

I'm starting to smile when Sophie bumps me again. We're about three blocks from the leotard store and a few doors down from Blue Skies when she tells me she wants taffy.

We duck under the Blue Skies sign and look in the window, where Sky and Blu are setting out some new magazines. Sky looks up and waves, and then Blu points to something behind us and we turn around.

A group of protesters are marching around in capes with white paint on their faces. They're carrying signs that say BAN THE BOMB and NEVER AGAIN with pictures of the mushroom cloud that exploded over Hiroshima. Sky told us about that because he and Blu go to a lot of marches to ban the bomb. He says they dropped it over Hiroshima and Nagasaki, two cities in Japan, and most everyone died and we should protest it whenever we can. If we don't, they'll build more bombs and those will be a hundred million times worse.

Sophie dashes over and I follow, and when one of the protestors sees us he holds out a sign and I take it. Sophie picks up another one and an older lady in a kerchief asks if we want makeup. Sophie lifts up her glasses and the lady puts this white stuff on Sophie's cheeks and starts rubbing it in. My friend picks up a sign and we start marching.

"Ban the bomb! Ban the bomb! Stop the killing and ban the bomb!"

Sky and Blu come out on the sidewalk to watch and I realize we're starting to draw a crowd. Someone holds out a petition and a couple of people sign it. I see Sky giving us a thumbs-up sign and a few more people walk over and then Blu starts waving frantically and I wave back.

Only now I see she's waving and pointing at something—but by the time I realize what she's pointing at, it's too late to run.

The angry sound of a siren cuts through the protesters' voices as a squad car pulls up to the curb. We all keep marching as though nothing is happening and the lady with the makeup smiles. "Don't worry," she says. "This happens all the time." The chants continue as Sophie grabs my arm, staring at the cop car. "Don't move," I whisper. "Just hold the sign up and stay behind it. Okay? No matter what."

"But Ru—"

"And don't act like you know me."

The car door opens and a woman gets out, slamming the door behind her. My heart sinks: it's Levitt. The chants grow louder and Sophie looks like she's going to cry. I realize everyone thinks the police are here for the protest; I'm the only one who knows they're not. I try to hide behind my sign but I'm pretty sure I've been spotted. "Over here, Flo," Levitt says, and I can tell by the sound of her voice that she's none too pleased.

5
Blue Skies

I LOOK BACK at Sophie once and shake my head. All of a sudden Mrs. Levitt is practically looming over us, and Sophie holds her sign out in front of both of us.

"Excuse me," Mrs. Levitt says to Sophie. "I need to bring your friend inside the store over there." Sophie looks like she wants to say something but I stare daggers at her and for once, she clams up. Mrs. Levitt, meanwhile, marches me across the street and up to the counter where Sky is combing his beard with his fingers. He always does that when he's nervous, and I can tell he's really nervous right now.

"What's goin' on, honey?" Sky asks.

"This is Mrs. Levitt. She's a social worker."

"Oh," says Sky. He stops combing his beard and leans forward. "What can I do for you?"

"Well, Mister—"

"Skylar," he says, holding out his hand. Mrs. Levitt doesn't take it.

"We got a tip today, Mr. Skylar."

"Oh?"

"Someone says you're running some kind of school? And this young lady goes to it?"

"I go to a real school, too," I say. Sky looks at me sharply.

"Which one?" Mrs. Levitt asks.

"P.S. 41," I tell her, which makes Sky's face go pale.

"I'll check the records on Monday, Ruby," Mrs. Levitt says, when Sky interrupts.

"We do have some classes here, Miss—"

"Levitt," she says, and all of a sudden Blu is at the counter, looking about as serious as you can look while holding *Mad* magazine. Blu has what Nell-mom calls a "husky" voice, and when she laughs you can hear it for miles. It's a great laugh really, the kind that comes straight from the belly and seems to go perfectly with her honey-colored hair and eyes. But right now Blu isn't laughing. She's staring at Mrs. Levitt, who is looking around the store.

I can tell she doesn't approve of the magazines. Some have painted covers like they were done by an artist—those are the poetry ones. Comics and motorcycle magazines fill another wall. A motorcycle is what Ray wants when he's older so he can bike across the country like they do in *The Wild One*.

Ray is crazy about motorcycles. I can't afford a real bike but said I'd spring for some magazines on his birthday. If I ever get out of this.

Mrs. Levitt turns around, and I try to see what she's looking at. There are bins full of ribbon candy and chocolate drops but I don't think she cares for those. Do social workers ever eat candy, or are they all too worried about cavities?

Posters of famous actors are on all the walls, like Brando, James Dean, Sophia Loren, and my favorite, Natalie Wood. The girls around here all want to look like her, but Blu says by the time we're old enough for that there'll be somebody else on the wall, somebody better. I don't really believe her because no one could be better than my Natalie.

Now Mrs. Levitt is leaning backward, looking at a row of green footprints that lead downstairs, where we have class.

"What is she learning here?"

Mrs. Levitt is asking Blu, who is looking at Sky, who is looking at me. Then Blu starts telling her. "Poetry, numbers, history—"

"What kind of history?"

"All kinds—"

"American? European?" Levitt asks.

"Both," says Blu. "We talk about the wars—"

"Which wars?"

"The World War. Korean War—"

"Does she have textbooks?"

"Textbooks?" Blu pauses and looks at me. Levitt looks at the policeman with a little smirk like she knows the jig is up.

"We use all kinds of books," Blu says finally.

"Well," Mrs. Levitt tells her, "if you don't use textbooks, this is not a school."

"We have a couple here somewhere," Sky says, but when Mrs. Levitt asks him where they are, the only one he can find is an old math book we used when I was seven.

"If Ruby isn't in school, she's truant," Levitt says. "And if her mother knows she's truant, then she's liable. And that could mean Ruby shouldn't be living with her."

"What?" I say, and my voice sounds high and reedy, even to me.

"You need to be cared for properly," Levitt replies, and all of a sudden my heart skips, whoosh, right into my throat, because I think she's talking about what happened to Nell-mom, which is a foster family.

Once you get in there, you don't get out so easily. So I'd not only have to leave my family, but Gordy, Sophie, and everyone else here, and probably never have another shot at seeing Kerouac. Not to mention having to go to a school and wear a uniform and have real homework with teachers who can hit you. God knows I'd never see Solange again.

"Hold on a minute," Sky says. "What if this is a real school?"

"You need to prove it," says Mrs. Levitt, turning to the policeman, who's been quiet all this time. "Isn't that right, officer?"

"You bet," he says, giving Sky and Blu the once-over like he wants to arrest them.

"Schools are accredited," Levitt is saying. "They're registered with the state of New York to teach certain subjects, which do not include the kind of poetry—"

"What's wrong with poetry?" Sky asks.

"That depends on what kind of poetry you're teaching," Levitt says. "Emily Dickinson and Shakespeare are fine, but some of the other people I see here—"

"What people?" Blu asks.

"One of your magazines features Allen Ginsberg," Levitt says, and I'm not kidding about the word "*features*." Then I hear her say, "Beyond the standards we set for decency."

"And whose standards are those?" Blu asks in a tight, hard voice.

"The standards of the state of New York," Mrs. Levitt answers. "Which mandates tests every year to be sure you meet them."

"I see," Sky says.

"Do you?" the policeman says. Sky looks like he wants to say something back, but Blu puts a hand on his arm.

"Not exactly," she says.

"Any student who goes here will have to pass a test," says Mrs. Levitt, "and you have until June to prepare for it."

"What happens if they don't?" says Blu.

Mrs. Levitt smiles. "Well now, look. I think you know the answer, don't you?"

Blu doesn't say anything.

"Look," Levitt says. "I know Beatniks have trouble with authority—"

"We don't call ourselves Beatniks—"

"Whatever you call yourselves. You do."

"Okay, fine," says Blu, narrowing her eyes. She has a really hard time when anyone tells her to do something, which I guess is what authority means, and most of the time, I agree with her. But right now it's my head on the block and if Levitt doesn't get what she wants I could be leaving the neighborhood. Which Blu knows of course, but it's like she can't help herself.

"What I have trouble with is people coming into our lives and making decisions."

"Honey," Sky starts saying, but Blu is on a roll.

"Which is why we all came down here in the first place," she says. "To get away from people like YOU holding up hoops and making us jump through them—"

"HONEY! BLU!" Sky shouts, and Blu finally starts to calm down. "Okay, fine," she says, "we'll pass your stupid test. You tell me what it is and she'll pass it."

"Very good," Levitt replies. "I'll be back this week with the standards. And you're right, there are hoops to jump through. If you don't agree, you can go to court and challenge us. But until you do and until you win that challenge, you still need to play by our rules. Is that clear?"

Blu looks at Levitt for a long time, and for a second I think she's going to slap her.

"Can you get out of my store now?" Blu says, and Sky starts combing his beard again.

"Be happy to," says Mrs. Levitt, and I start thinking she's going to turn and leave. Instead she looks at Sky. "Anyone else go to your school?"

Before Sky can answer, Blu looks right at her and says, "If you have any more questions I'm going to get a lawyer."

Mrs. Levitt doesn't say anything, but she puts a hand on my shoulder. "Well. You and I, young lady, have another stop to make, don't we?"

I look up at her, wondering what would happen if I double over and pretend to be sick. Except Levitt seems to be onto me, because she leans over and whispers, "Don't even think about it."

I look at her dead on, trying not to blink. She straightens up and says, "You, me, and the officer, Ruby, are going on a walk right now. We still have to see your mom—provided you have one."

If only I didn't—just this once.

6
Little Nell's

POETRY ISN'T really good for anything except making you feel better. That's why it's art. If it was good for something, it would be useful and practical, like a cooking pot or a bicycle. If it's not, it must be there for some other reason, but it might not be something you can name. Right now I'm using it to keep from panicking, which I seem to be doing a lot of lately. The problem is if you don't write it down you may not remember what you're thinking. But I don't think Mrs. Levitt is going to wait for me to pull out my notebook, so all I can do is try out the words in my head.

> *The crowd snakes and weaves*
> *Like the Great Wall of China*
> *On a cab ride*

Out on a Saturday
Sunny with arms and chins
All moving at eye level and they all
Have a Somewhere as they go.

I look around for Sophie but she must have scattered with the rest of the protesters. We cross West Seventh and head over to Waverly, with me leading the way. Little Nell's building is all lit up with artists coming and going, and she's on the highest floor. I'm taking the stairs as slow as I can to give myself time to figure out what to say when I get in the studio. I'm also trying to figure out what painting Nell-mom is working on and how Mrs. Levitt will see it.

There's a picture of a horse, because Nell-mom likes horses. If you look at it one way it's sort of old-fashioned, what they call a tableau. The horse is pulling a buggy down Bleecker Street and it's a long time ago, like another century. Only the horse is kind of transparent and the people in the buggy are really skeletons.

Another painting was started a week ago. It's all halves of things, half women eating half fruits in half chairs. I'm not sure if Nell-mom's done with it because I think she wants to leave it half-finished.

My favorite is the canvas she painted black, with a red stripe down the middle ending in splatters down to the edge. Most of her paintings don't have names but that one is *Life*. Nell-mom is also working on a basket of apples, but I don't think they'd appeal to a social worker because they're all withered and wormy, in a basket of blood. Some even have faces that look like they're screaming.

I'm not sure which one of these paintings we're going to see but as soon as we set foot in the studio— me, Levitt, and the policeman—I wish I'd brought them somewhere else. Instead of a painting with bloody apples or gashes, we see Nell-mom painting a man with no clothes on, holding a saxophone. Even worse, Ray is watching them, his fingers dancing in the air like he's trying to show the man how to play.

The man turns his face as we get closer and I recognize him by his mustache, which is dark and bristly. He owns a gallery on Charles Street and sometimes buys one of Nell-mom's paintings. They were friends in high school, but not in a romantic way, and I think his name was Charlie then. When they came out here, he changed his name to Chaz. I'm guessing Nell-mom doesn't have to pay him, but other than that I can't see why she'd want to paint him in his birthday suit.

Nell-mom's face is spattered with orange and green. She's got a streak of yellow in her hair, and her fingers look like she dipped them in blood. She's concentrating on her painting so hard, and Ray is so busy explaining the saxophone, that neither one of them sees us coming. Nell-mom is all hunched over because the studio's in an attic and the ceiling is sloped. When she looks up—*BANG!*—her head collides with the ceiling.

"Are you okay?" I ask.

Her face is as white as a sheet. "Ruby?" Nell-mom yelps.

"Ohhhh!" Mrs. Levitt puts her hands over my eyes as soon as she sees Chaz.

"What's going on?" says Nell-mom.

"I'm Gayle Levitt. I work for the state," Mrs. Levitt tells her. "Is this your daughter?"

"Of course she's my daughter! What is this?"

"She was caught stealing today," Mrs. Levitt says. "And she tried to run away from us. That's why the officer is here."

"I wasn't stealing!" I say, pushing Mrs. Levitt's hands away.

"Stealing what?" Nell-mom asks.

"Outside a fruit stand."

Nell's mouth drops open.

"We understand your daughter doesn't go to school."

"Of course she does!" Nell cries.

"She goes to a store called Blue Skies. And we don't really know what she's doing there."

Nell-mom looks from me to Ray and back at me again.

"You're not aware of this?" asks Mrs. Levitt.

"Of course I am," Nell-mom says.

"And who is this young man?"

"I'm her son," Ray answers, and Mrs. Levitt shakes her head.

"Your son?" Mrs. Levitt's voice sounds a little tighter than it was a minute ago. "And why are you here?"

"I was bringing her lunch," says Ray. "And then she thought—she asked for the saxophone."

"I see," Mrs. Levitt says. "But should you really be here when there's a man with no—hmmm." She clears her throat.

"Now, Levitt," says the policeman. "At least he ain't totally in the buff. I mean, he's got, you know. His horn."

I guess we're all supposed to laugh at this, but of course nobody does.

"It's not a horn," says Ray. "It's a saxophone."

"Oh really?" the policeman says.

"It's played with a reed," Ray says. "I mean, a sax is a woodwind, okay? It's not like a trumpet."

"Oh yeah?" the policeman says. He looks like he's about to bust out laughing but Ray doesn't notice. He's just going on about woodwinds like that's the most important thing in the world. "So if you can't dig that—"

"I can dig it!" says the policeman. "What I can't dig is if there's any kind of indecency in a public place."

"What are you talking about?" Nell-mom scowls. "I'm painting a model and my son is showing him how to hold the saxophone. And this is not a public place. It's a studio and people are painting in them all over the city!"

"And you think it's proper for a child to be in here?" Levitt says.

"He's fourteen and I'm not—this is an artistic rendering," Nell-mom sputters.

"Well, let's just say I question it, shall we? Your daughter wanders the streets stealing apples and doesn't go to school, and—"

"I keep telling you I don't steal!" I say, but no one is listening to me.

"By the way," says Mrs. Levitt, "where does your son go?"

"Frankly it's none of your business. We have a right to teach them at home," says Nell-mom.

"But they're not at home, are they? My concern is for these children and what kind of life they're leading."

"I don't need your concern," Nell tells her. "My children are just fine."

"How about this?" Mrs. Levitt replies. "I'd like to visit you at home this week to be sure they're being treated properly. They also need to be tested by the state so we know they're being educated in compliance with state guidelines. Are you in Monday?"

"No," says Nell-mom.

"Not even late in the afternoon?" Mrs. Levitt asks.

"I don't—I'll have to let you know."

"Well." Mrs. Levitt hands Nell-mom a card with her name and phone number printed on it. "Give me a call Monday morning, all right? I can always stop by in the evening if you work during the day."

She turns away, nearly colliding with the policeman, who is staring at Nell-mom.

"By the way, *are* you a missus?" he asks.

Nell-mom doesn't answer and after a minute, Levitt turns to leave and the policeman follows her. It's so quiet in the studio, we can hear the *clickety-clack* of Mrs. Levitt's shoes as she walks down the hall to the stairwell. And then Nell-mom looks at me.

"Don't worry," I tell her. "I gave her the wrong address."

Nell-mom shakes her head slowly, but doesn't say anything. I keep thinking she ought to be screaming or at least turning purple but she's just staring at me and I'm getting the weirdest feeling. It's like when Gary Daddy-o had a fight with her and left for two days, and we had no idea where he was or where to find him. Instead of crying or yelling, she just sat and stared out the window, or paced up and down the hall. It was like a silent movie with people moving and no sound.

And here I am doing the one thing I was told never to do, which is to get "the man" involved in our lives; we call it "the man," but it's the state or boss man or anyone who has the power to make you miserable. But all Nell-mom can do is stand there while Chaz gets off the platform and says, to no one in particular, "Maybe I better get dressed."

Nobody answers him, so after a few seconds he hands Ray his saxophone and goes behind a screen in the back of the room. I look at Nell-mom and then at the floor. I want to tell her how all I did was touch an apple I had no intention of stealing, and how Tattoo Tina set the whole thing up because she hates me, but for some reason my throat feels tight and when I try to talk, it's like I swallowed a block of wood.

I wish Nell-mom would bark at me or throw something. But instead she starts blinking like she's trying not to cry, and then her mouth is trembling and she turns and runs out of the room. All I can do is look at the paintbrush she left on her easel, dripping paint all over the floor. I should probably clean it, but I just stand there with my hands in my pockets, trying to remember the lines I made up on the way over here. I sort of do but don't, really. I try to start over again.

> *Crowds. Weaving.*
> *Sunny Saturday.*
> *Filling streets in a weave of colors*
> *Like a snakeskin up-and-down*
> *breathing*
> *Going where?*
> *But there is nowhere*

If Nell-mom is crying, it means I messed up really bad. If she doesn't know how to fix it, then it might be it can't be fixed. I try not to think about it, see if I can get somewhere with "Sunny Saturday." But the words won't come.

7
Maybe

WHEN NELL-MOM was a kid, her mother picked her up after school to bring her to the antique shop their family owned in Sheboygan, Wisconsin. There wasn't much to do there but the couches were cool, if you judge by the pictures in our living room. They had a red velvet sofa with big, rounded arms that came from a saloon in the 1800s before Sheboygan was a town. But on this particular day, Little Nell and her mother were on the way to their shop because there was a shipment coming, and no time to spare.

They were in a big black car like you see in old pictures of the 1930s, and there was a song on the radio called "Makin' Whoopee!" Nell had just got her report card and she was telling her mother all her grades, and her little brother Eric was in the backseat jumping up and down begging for ice cream. They were on a two-lane road going into town and there was a farmer in front of them driving a cart and he was going slowly, like a tortoise on its back, Nell's mother said. And the size of his cart made it really hard to see around him.

Nell remembers what was on the radio because when her mother decided to pass, she was also yelling at Eric to be quiet and puffing on her cigarette and didn't see the car in the other lane and as soon as she got up by the farmer, they were hit and Nell heard "Whoopee!" and then a tremendous *BANG!* and she jerked forward into the windshield.

When Nell woke up in the hospital, they said she would have a tiny scar on her forehead but no one would notice it and she was very, very lucky and Eric was lucky, too. The only one who wasn't lucky was Nell's mother, who would never be able to walk again, not even with a cane. That meant her father had to close down the store and work on the railroad, so his kids wouldn't see him very much. Nell and Eric had to live with their grandmother, who was mostly okay but drank a lot so they were always late to school.

Their teacher complained, of course, so the social worker got involved, and Nell and her brother went to a foster home. Their foster mother made the kids sleep with their hands outside the covers, so they couldn't do anything naughty, she said. They couldn't even put their hands under the blankets when it was cold.

The last day Nell-mom was in her grandmother's house was her birthday. I think she was turning nine, and I'm trying to remember how old her brother was, when I realize Chaz is talking to me. "What happened to your mother?"

"Um, she had to go."

I'm not sure why Nell-mom wanted to paint him. He's a little paunchy and his hair's going gray, so his mustache looks kind of weird in comparison. I know gallery owners like to check out the art scene, and that may be what he's doing here. I just wish he hadn't been doing it today.

"Is she okay?" says Chaz. "She's not upset, is she? Wow."

Before I can answer, he rushes out of the studio. Then Ray looks at me and says, "You really did it, Ruby."

"Yeah," I say. "Thanks."

"Come on. Let's get out of here."

"You go," I tell him. "I need to clean up."

He stands in the doorway trying to decide what he should do.

"I got stuck in a closet today," I say.

"What?" I tell him about trying to ditch Mrs. Levitt and meeting the Soroccos.

"Sounds kind of funny," he says, smiling.

"Not to me."

"I don't know why they got all crazy in here. I mean artists paint this stuff all the time. What's the big deal?"

How do boys get so dumb? Do they, like, study for it or something?

"You and me," I tell him. "*We're* the big deal."

"Don't worry about it," he says. "It'll be okay."

It's really hard getting Ray to worry. He's a lot like Gary Daddy-o, who says while everything matters, nothing matters very much. I think that's another one of those Zen sayings. What it really means is if you want to get through life without falling apart, you can't let every flippy little thing get to you. Gary Daddy-o is so Zen that when he and Nell-mom fight, he lies down on the floor and stops talking. After a while, she'll sit down next to him and they'll start laughing or something. Once in a while, she'll just storm out, but that's how it goes because being in love is no romance. At least that's what Nell-mom says.

"Want me to wait for you?" Ray asks.

"Nah." I pick up a bottle of turpentine and pour it into a cup to clean the brushes. Ray nods and after watching for a little bit, he goes.

It feels good to be doing something, even if all I'm doing is swirling red and black streaks through my fingers, watching the brushes turn soft and brown. Nell-mom will be too upset to make dinner, so Ray will have cereal but I'm really tired of Cheerios. If

Gary Daddy-o gets home before dark, he'll either grab a hot dog on the way or eat at Les and Bo's if they're playing music together. I think he's going on tour tomorrow in Philadelphia and if Nell-mom tells him what happened he'll be going out on a "sour note." That's what he likes to say when we mess up.

I look up at the clock on the wall. What if I were to show up at Les and Bo's, too? If Gary Daddy-o's there, I can tell him my side of the story and if he's not, I can at least get something to eat. On weekends, they order Chinese food or cook something Oriental. It takes me about a minute to realize the clock doesn't work and I have no idea what time it is. By now, I'm so hungry I could eat gum wrappers.

By the time I get downstairs, the streets are crowding up with weekend people and it takes almost half an hour to get to Christopher Street. Les and Bo live in the tallest building on the block. It has glass doors and a tiny hallway with buzzers, mailboxes, and a second door leading to the stairs. I push the doorbell and wait. One, two, three, nothing. Nobody's home.

I'm halfway outside when all of a sudden I hear *buzzzzz*. I grab for the inside door, but I'm too late and the buzzing stops. I ring again and when the buzzer sounds, I push open the door. I hear a trumpet and someone else on the drums before I even get upstairs. A woman with a cigarette dangling out of her mouth opens the door and points to my shoes. You always have to take them off before they let you in.

At least fifty zillion people are inside but the pulse of the music is so strong it just pulls at me. This is it, I'm thinking, the heart of the Beat world and it's here at Les and Bo's. It's like they put their hands around the city's throat and squeezed, and all the life came up into their apartment. Les is playing his sax by the window, facing the street so all I see is the dragon on the back of his red kimono. He has white-gold hair worn Roman-style and a chain around his neck. Bo is playing jazz riffs on guitar, shaking his head from side to side. He's from Alabama and calls himself an Authentic American African. I just call him Bo.

The rug feels really good on my feet, thick and soft. I look around for Gary Daddy-o but can't find him. Then I see Ray, right next to Les and staring like he's hypnotized, with fingers twitching like he's playing the same notes. I guess he didn't want to go home either. Les has been teaching Ray on sax for the past three years and says one of these days Ray will be good enough to play at the Village Gate. Right now, he's so wrapped up in Les's playing he doesn't even see me—but I don't mind.

There are cartons of Chinese food around the living room and everyone's spooning it onto paper plates. Someone hands me a plate piled high with rice and pork and I wolf it down, but when I look around for something to drink all I see is red wine. I'm so thirsty I go into the bathroom and lean over the sink, scooping water into my mouth from the tap. When I come out, I see plates of pistachio ice cream. I'd never put pistachios in ice cream but I guess that's what's cool about it.

A couple of guys roll up the rug and people start dancing as the drums get louder, pulling at my sleeves and hair and everything else on me to move or sing or dance. I close my eyes for a minute, just listening to the sounds around me. It could be New York, but it sounds more like Africa.

> *Every spring*
> *They sprout like toadstools*
> *In the key of heat*
> *Over Egypt and Khartoum and the rain*
> *in Brazil*
> *Drum rain beating on the heads of*
> *birds*
> *And umbrellas while the sky goes*
> *Clean white empty trumpet beating*
> *RED out of the sky*
> *And we're moving into it or is the*
> *beat moving us*

"Yeah?" I hear someone say.
What?
"Keep going."

I'm sitting on the stoop outside Les and Bo's with no idea how I got there. And a guy is sitting there looking at me. Was I talking out loud? I feel my cheeks go hot. "I'm . . . I don't know. Just—"

"It's okay," he says. "What's your name?"

His face is tough and leathery like a wolf and he has dark hair and eyes and a black leather jacket. Not Kerouac, but . . . could be. Almost? For some reason I'm blanking on his name. Guy? Gil? I could swear I saw him outside The Scene.

If he's who I think he is, he grew up here in the Village. Why can't I remember his name?

They have these contests at The Scene. The poets stand up one by one and say their best poems, and the winner gets a pot of money and sometimes gets his book published. I think this guy won the night I walked by The Scene because they were carrying him out on their shoulders, shouting and singing.

It has to be him but I can't ask.

"Okay, don't tell me," he says.

"No, just—sorry," I say. "I must have come down here—I was looking for my notebook."

He nods and reaches into his shirt pocket, pulling out a pack of cigarettes. Then he reaches behind his back and gets a notebook, holding it out to me.

"Hey, thanks." I take the notebook.

Gregory. Gregory Corso? That would be unbelievable. Even I wouldn't believe it. Corso handing me a notebook so I can write a poem?

They say he lived with his uncle and ran away all the time and for a while, he was in prison. That's where he fell in love with poetry and turned into a writer.

"Are you—"

"No."

"No?"

"Not who you think I am," he says.

"Gregory—"

"That's what you think?"

I look at him, trying to decide.

"Well, are you?"

"Maybe."

"Yeah?"

"Maybe not."

"Well," I say, "I'm not who you think I am either."

"But you do have a name, don't you?"

"Ruby."

"Ruby, huh? Nice name."

I don't say anything. I'm still trying to figure out who he is.

"So, Ruby. You gonna finish that poem or not?"

I open the notebook and see his handwriting, scrawling over the pages. I want to read all of them but of course I can't, so I flip through instead until I find a blank page. My poem is sounding dumber and dumber the more I think about it, but if a cat like that hands you a notebook you have no choice but to write it down. I try to remember what I was saying, and more important, what it felt like at Les and Bo's. When I'm done writing, I look up to see him staring out at the street.

He looks over at me.

"Read it."

I think, are you kidding? Are you nuts?

"Come on, Ruby. Read it to me."

This can't be happening, just can't be. Famous people don't just talk to kids. Do they?

"It's not ready," I say.

He turns away without answering and pulls out a cigarette.

I want to ask him to read something of his but how can I? This is all just so weird. I skim through his notebook, trying not to let him see. But I can tell he's looking at me.

The sound of drums rolls out from a window somewhere above us and my heart starts beating fast.

"Anyway," I say. "I—don't mean to bug you."

And then it gets even weirder because he holds out his hand, and I give him the notebook. Then he opens it.

And reads.

8
Silky

I REALLY SHOULDN'T call it reading because it's more like he starts speaking silk to me. Not French, not English, not anything you'd recognize. Just a whole other language, skimming the air between us like a banner.

There's something about India and the fingernail of Malaya, and then the Korea Ti-Pousse Thumb, whatever that is. Salamanders, Moon Spots, the backs of mountains, kines, and balconies (kines?). It's a road poem, but more like a bird is writing it; through Nebraska, Atlantis, and swans of balls, which sounds like it should be "ball of swans" but isn't.

I want to look up kine and Ti-Pousse Thumb, but we don't have a dictionary at home and I have to wait until Monday to see the one at Blue Skies. I can't ask what it means because I don't want to look stupid—but I'm starting to wonder if Corso really did write this poem.

I want to say Kerouac wrote it but I know this guy isn't him. I mean, he just doesn't . . . look like Kerouac. He's too . . . I don't know. His eyes aren't big enough and he doesn't have those boots, not the ones I think Kerouac wears. In fact, he's wearing sneakers and they have lots of holes in them.

"Now it's your turn." He closes the notebook.

"I told you I'm not ready."

"Just tell me something," he says. "I don't care what it is."

If he would only tell me his name. But I'm starting to think he gets asked a lot and doesn't want to say. It has to be Gregory Corso. Just does.

I tell him about the fruit store and Little Nell and Mrs. Levitt, and he seems like he's really listening, even though people are snaking around the stairs the whole time going into Les and Bo's.

"Well, hey," he says. "That's rough."

"Tell me about it!"

"You like poetry?" he asks. "I mean writing it."

"Well—yeah, I mean, I'm not a real poet—like you," I say.

"How do you know?"

"Well, I mean—I don't know—"

The door behind us opens, and a blond in black pedal pushers and a sleeveless leotard pokes her head out. Her hair is teased up high in a beehive and she has long, dangly earrings like a movie star. "There you are," she says, smiling. One of her front teeth is chipped but that doesn't make her look bad. In fact, it makes her more interesting.

Maybe-Gregory doesn't answer but that doesn't seem to bother her. She eyes me up and down, scoots over, and wraps herself around him.

I turn away and get up, thinking I'll go back inside.

"Where you off to?" he asks.

The woman buries her head in his neck.

"I don't know," I say. "I've got to find my brother."

"Lou," he says. "This is Ruby."

She doesn't say anything.

"Got the man on her tail," he says. "Trying to make her go to school."

Lou glances at me, not like she's interested or anything, but trying to pretend she is to make him happy. "Oh yeah?"

"I'm tryin' to help her out here. So she won't have to go."

"What d'you mean?" Lou asks, wrinkling up her nose. "Doesn't she have to?"

"She learns over at Blue Skies."

"Blue Skies?"

"Here's what I'd do," Maybe-Gregory says. But then he doesn't say anything.

"What?" I say.

"Like Gandhi," he says. "Yeah."

"Gandhi?"

"Like he would, like . . . a hunger strike."

"She can't do that," Lou says. "She's just a kid."

"She can if she has to," he says.

"Didn't you go to school?" I ask.

"I did when I had to. But what you need is something else," he says. "They call it a cause célèbre."

"A what?"

"You get all these people behind you. Make sure everyone knows about it and people read about you in the paper. Then the social workers have to back down."

"Why would they want to read about me?"

"A kid your age on a hunger strike? They'll be crazy for it. And you'll have that lady running."

"Yeah, but—how long would I have to go without eating?"

"Long as it takes."

I can barely go a minute.

"You can have water," he says.

Great.

I run my hands along the banister, thinking about Gandhi. Sky told us about him once, which I only remember because he was playing a record from India. I know that's where Gandhi is from and that he was pretty much the reason India got to be independent. I think it was because he was always on a hunger strikes, but how did he do it? They don't get a lot to eat in countries like that anyway, so maybe he was used to it.

Lou seems to be done pretending she's even interested. She nibbles at Maybe-Gregory's ear like it's a cookie and I rub my eyes, looking out at the street. By now all the streetlamps are on, and the music floating from the windows above us is getting louder.

"Doin' anything on April 12?" Maybe-Gregory asks.

"Me?"

"Yeah, you," he says.

I don't want to tell him it's my birthday. So I just ask him why.

"We're doing a reading at Chumley's."

That's the bar by the Edna St. Vincent Millay House. It was a speakeasy during Prohibition when you couldn't have liquor because it was against the law. So you went there if you wanted alcohol. I have no idea why they call it a speakeasy, except maybe it was easy to ask for a drink. There's no sign on the door and they still have a tiny glass window so people can check you out before letting you inside.

"I can get you in," he says. "If you want."

Is this really happening? A Beat poet is inviting me to a reading on my birthday. Could I really go to Chumley's? I try to imagine Sophie's face when I tell her. She's absolutely going to die.

"Oh, yeah. Sure," I say like it was nothing, but my heart's going so fast I'm sure he can hear it. Could I really get in that place? What do I tell Nell and Gary Daddy-o? Can I get Ray to take me? Or just close the door of my room and sneak out?

"Come on home with me, baby," Lou is saying, and this time the guy looks like he might be listening.

"Um—what time?" I say.

"Don't know," he says. "Just—night."

Lou pulls him to his feet and he waves, following behind her as she pulls him downstairs. The door opens, and four or five people come out holding beer cans. I know Ray is still upstairs but Gary Daddy-o probably went home and by the time I see him, he'll already have heard everything from Little Nell.

You'll have to go to school, she'll say. You'll have to do whatever they want. And if they think we're bad parents, there's nothing we can do.

A cause célèbre, I think, but there's got to be something better than a hunger strike. But what am I talking about? I just met someone amazing and he read me his poetry. He might know Kerouac, too. Of course he knows him. And he invited me to Chumley's! Which would make Levitt crazy, of course. When you pass by and they open the door, the smell of beer is so strong it's like you're drinking it. That would melt her, I think, like the witch in *The Wizard of Oz*. But of course, she won't melt, which means I've got to think of something.

I sit on the stoop again, leaning against the banister. I've had some doozies in my life but this is the craziest.

And even crazier, that poem I just wrote?

It's in this guy's notebook. So if I want to remember it exactly like I wrote it, I *have* to go to the reading.

Right?

9
Remember This

GRIMY. DARK. Sticky floor and rotting garbage.
Levitt is writing notes to herself, swiveling her head
as she moves through our house from one room to
the next. She thinks I don't know what she's writing
but I can see every word. Nell-mom is sitting at the
kitchen table tugging at her hair, which is what she
always does when she's nervous. She was supposed
to do the dishes this morning but I guess she forgot,
and I've been at Blue Skies all day so I couldn't get
to them either. But dishes are the least of it.

Someone told Levitt where we lived, which made
her pretty mad to begin with because she figured
out I gave her the wrong address. She came in here
looking for trouble and from her point of view, I
guess, it's easy to find it. I think Ray spilled syrup
this morning, and the kitchen floor is so sticky you

can barely put your foot down without losing the sole of your shoe. No one's taken out the garbage for a few days and of course Ray has to leave a trail of clothes wherever he goes.

That's the grimy part and there's also a dark part— but that one's not our fault. If you're facing the back alley it's going to be dark, because the windows are narrow. That's the way they liked them in the nine- teenth century when this place was probably built.

Levitt's found her way into the bathroom. She looks up at the ceiling, which is cracked and peel- ing, and at the rusty smudges in the toilet and tub. The faucet is going *drip, drip, drip,* so I reach over and turn it off. That helps a little. Now we're off to the bedrooms. Mine is the smallest in the house and looks even smaller because it's black. It barely has room for a bed and dresser so I share the hall closet with my mom. I think it's the coolest room in the house because it looks out over a cobblestone walk and has a poster of Natalie Wood and James Dean in *Rebel without a Cause,* leaning in close like they're about to kiss.

Ray's room is bigger but he's older and you know how that goes. Besides it's not all that big and has clothes and sheet music everywhere. It's like the rest of the house has little pockets of Ray, and then this is the Ray CENTER, where everything he's ever worn or touched is all over the place, like it's been through a Ray Volcano.

Now Levitt's in the front room where Nell-mom and Gary Daddy-o sleep. There's a chair, closet, and foldout sofa, plus a dresser in the corner by the radiator. It's funny how something can look pretty good until you see it with someone else's eyes.

I'm looking at the cream-colored shawl draped over the couch with a row of fringes along the bottom half. It has bright red roses wrapped in green leaves, and when Nell-mom is in a good mood she drapes it around her waist and dances flamenco with Gary Daddy-o. But Levitt doesn't see the shawl. She's looking at the worn-out cushions and the spot where Solange threw up on the rug. She pulls out her notebook and scribbles something in it and the way she scribbles makes me want to shiver. I'd hate to read that notebook cover to cover, with all the notes about dirty dishes and rusty toilet bowls. But I know someone is reading it every day.

She turns to me. "Where is your brother, Ruby?"

"How should I know?"

"Do you know, Mrs.—Miss—"

Levitt walks into the kitchen again, looking at Nell-mom, who still isn't talking.

"Mrs.," I say.

"Yes. Well—by the way. I meant to ask you—"

"Excuse me," Nell-mom says, unfolding her long legs and standing up. Levitt watches her expectantly but Nell-mom won't even look at her. Instead, she goes into the bathroom, shutting the door.

"Well," Levitt says, looking at me.

"Well what?"

She folds her arms and stares at the floor. "You know, Ruby, I haven't been on this job very long. In fact, I only started a few months ago."

I feel my heart pounding and remind myself to breathe, nice and easy. "Yeah?"

"So I want to be sure I'm doing the right thing, you know what I mean? Because I know . . . you love your mom and your mom loves you. I just want— you know it's my job to be sure you're safe."

"Well, you can see I am," I say.

"Really, Ruby? Are you sure?" Her eyes widen as she leans over and touches my cheek, and I can see her hands are shaking. For a split second I think she really cares about me. But instead of making me feel better, it makes me feel worse.

"Listen," I say, stepping back and away from Levitt. "I have to take out the garbage."

"That's a good idea," Levitt says. "Can I help you?"

I don't answer and pull the bag out from under the sink. It's full to overflowing and I have to walk slowly so it doesn't fall apart. Levitt holds the door open so I can bring it outside and watches me dump it in the can at the bottom of the stairs. I turn back and walk up again, and as she moves back to let me inside the house I feel she's relaxing a little, and it's going to be okay.

And it would have been.

Because you can't take someone's child away just because the house is a mess. But when Nell-mom comes out of the bathroom, Levitt is standing there, and something about the set of her mouth makes my heart start pounding again.

"How long have you and your husband been together?"

"What?"

"I said, how long have you been married?"

"I don't know."

"You don't know?" Levitt says.

"Thirteen years."

"And your boy is fourteen?"

"Fourteen years," says Nell-mom.

"You have a marriage license?"

"What?"

"Well, Mrs.—" Levitt squints at her notes. "Ta—what?"

"Tabeata," Nell-mom says. "T-a-b-e-a-t-a."

"In the phone book it says 'T-a-b-*i*-t-a.'"

Nell-mom smirks. "I don't care what it says."

"Okay," Levitt says. "And it seems you don't have a wedding ring."

"I don't like rings."

"I see. What about the license then?"

"What about it?"

"Oh, dear," Levitt sighs. Then Nell-mom turns to her, and by the look in her eye I can tell she's done being quiet. And that isn't good.

"Why are people so stuck on this?"

"What do you mean, 'stuck'?"

"We don't need a piece of paper."

Mrs. Levitt's face is getting redder and redder. "Are you telling me now that you are NOT married?"

"You knew that," Nell-mom replies. "I didn't have to tell you anything."

Mrs. Levitt writes that in her notebook and then looks up. "I did not know it," she says.

"We do everything married people do," Nell-mom continues. "We live together. We take care of each other. We take care of Ruby and Ray."

"But it's not really the same at all," Levitt says. "Nor is it the best example for your children. Have you thought about what they're learning here?"

Nell-mom folds her arms and shakes her head, like she does when she's mad at Gary Daddy-o.

"Not going to school, living in squalor—"

"You call this *squalor*?"

"It's not me, all right? It's what I see here—"

"She worked all day," I say. "She doesn't have time—"

But Levitt isn't listening. "It's just part and parcel, Ruby," she answers. "Part of everything that's wrong here. And the truth is I'm worried about you."

"Well, you can stop worrying," I say. "There's nothing wrong with me."

"You lie, you steal, you don't go to school, and your parents aren't married—"

"I never lied in my life—" I start to say but she puts her hands up and shakes her head.

"You lied about where you live."

She has me there.

"You know what?" Nell-mom says. "None of this is any of your business."

"I think you're wrong, Miss," Levitt says. "But I'm not out to get you here—"

Nell-mom walks over to the sink, turning her back to us. Because I've seen her like this before, I know that Nell-mom is about to get really, really mad. But I don't think Levitt knows it. And I can't help it. I start to get scared.

BANG! A dish flies across the room, and then another dish, and a glass.

"What—"

BANG! Solange jumps up from the windowsill and races out of the room.

"Mom—Nell-mom," I call out, but she isn't listening.

"Who ARE you?" Nell-mom screams. "Telling me WHAT I'M SUPPOSED TO DO?!"

"NELL-MOM!" Now I'm yelling, too, but it doesn't stop her. Three more glasses are broken and a cereal bowl goes *SPLAT!* onto the floor.

Mrs. Levitt is done talking. She grabs me by the hand and pulls me out of the kitchen so fast my feet barely skim across the floor. And then she pushes me toward the door.

"Come on—"

"You come on!" I say, shaking free.

"We're getting out of here—"

"YOU get out—"

"You are coming with me—"

"She is NOT coming with you." Now Nell-mom is standing in the doorway.

"I am taking this child out of here, and if you stop me I will call the police," says Levitt. I can see she's shaking pretty bad.

I look around for someone, anyone, to stop this from happening. But no one is there. Gary Daddy-o left for Philadelphia last night and Ray could be anywhere.

"NO!" Nell-mom is yelling, but by this time Levitt is ignoring her.

"I know you don't like this," she says. "But right now it's for the best."

"Nell-mom," I say, trying to get her to look at me.

Levitt answers instead: "Ruby. Listen."

I call to Nell-mom again, softly, but she's turned to block the front door and won't look my way.

"Look, Miss," Levitt is saying, "I assure you I will call the police."

"Well, you'll have to use someone else's phone," says Nell-mom, and then Levitt nods and looks at me.

"All right. Very good."

Levitt squishes past Nell-mom and scoots outside. I see her cross the street, walking with quick, determined steps to the phone booth on the corner. Meanwhile, Nell-mom starts pulling clothes out of drawers and packing—clothes, shoes, books, and pillows. "We're getting out of here, Ruby. Help me."

"What?" I say. Does Nell-mom really think she can get us packed and out the door before Levitt gets back? Two apples fly out of the refrigerator and a jar of peanut butter is shoved in a bag.

Nell-mom looks at me. "Money."

"Didn't Gary Daddy-o leave you some?"

"Are you kidding?"

"Will you get married like Mrs. Levitt says?"

"No," says Nell-mom. Her voice is flat.

"Why not?"

Her eyes narrow. "Just . . . can't."

"What do you mean?"

Nell-mom reaches into the refrigerator, then bangs it shut and straightens up. "It's not me, okay? This is your father's fault. ALL of it!"

"How can it be? He's not even here!"

"Exactly." Nell-mom scowls. "Can't be bothered with us."

What is she talking about? I don't understand. "But he's a musician. He's on the road—"

"I don't have time for this, Ruby! Come ON!" Nell-mom pulls a suitcase out of the closet and rushes through my room, sweeping up everything in sight. But I can't leave without Solange. Where is she? As I kneel to look under the couch, I can hear

Nell-mom sobbing, which tells me there's a police car outside. The next thing I know, they're pounding on the door.

I don't want to go like this, with dishes in pieces on the floor and my cat cowering under the sofa. I don't want to remember it, most of all.

"Ma'am?" the policeman calls as Mrs. Belusa leans out her window upstairs.

"Who is that?" she says. "What's happening?"

I want to remember that shawl on the couch, and Nell-mom dancing in it. I want to remember Ray playing "My Melancholy Baby" at night in his room, and Gary Daddy-o juggling oranges in the kitchen.

"I'll get her things together," Levitt is saying. "Just get her out of there."

I close my eyes and stick my fingers in my ears. I won't remember this. I refuse.

"Ruby." Nell-mom's voice sounds muffled and broken.

"Ma'am!" the policeman pounds harder on the door.

I try to tell them about Solange and Ray and Gary Daddy-o. I try to tell them about Nell-mom, how she paints iodine on my cuts in different shapes and calls them abstract art; how I know she doesn't mean to yell or get mad, and the only reason she's like this is because she's scared of social workers—with good reason.

But they're not even looking at me. Levitt sees the suitcase in my room and grabs it. She brings it down to the squad car while Solange, who has finally come out, jumps up on a shelf to watch.

They make me go with them, *boom-boom-boom* down the stairs while I hear Nell-mom calling my name as the neighbors rush out to gather around her. I watch her bending forward, the tendons standing out in her neck, and as the car pulls away I watch her mouth silently screaming and I close my eyes again.

I won't remember this. I won't remember this at all.

10
Regular Real

WE'RE ON THE top floor of what could either be an orphanage or asylum, but the sign outside says it's a children's home. There are just three girls in here, and before she leaves, Levitt tells me their names: Judy, Harriet, and Manuela. Judy is small with blue eyes and a worry line between them. Harriet is huge by comparison, a tomboy with jeans and dark brown hair in a pixie cut with bangs. Of the three, Manuela is dressed the nicest, with a white blouse and blue sweater. She has long, dark hair knotted into a braid that falls down to her waist. Right now, they're all staring at me.

"What's your name?"

"When d'you get here?"

"*Tú* are . . . okay?"

Manuela has an accent, but I can't tell where she's from. Normally I'd be curious, but I'm too upset to worry about it right now. I want to start on a hunger strike but don't know if I can last. Even if the food is terrible, I know I'm still going to get hungry. On the other hand, a kid who won't eat could be pretty upsetting to the people here—and like Gregory Corso said, that might be enough to get me out.

I decide to tell them my name, but instantly regret it because they want to know everything. I put my hand up and shake my head.

"Stop," says Manuela. "She doesn't want to talk about it."

"Like you know what she wants," says Harriet, and I glance upward to look at her more closely. From the way everyone's looking at her I can see she doesn't take arguments lightly.

"I know we shouldn't bug her," Manuela says, but no sooner are the words out of her mouth when Harriet shoves her. Manuela stumbles back against the wall.

"Hey!" I say.

"Hey, what?" Harriet asks.

"Leave her alone."

"Gonna make me?"

"Yeah," I say, getting up from the mattress I'm sitting on. The whole room is full of these thin, lumpy mattresses, except for three beds that have been made up.

"Be careful," Manuela calls out. "Harriet is strong."

Maybe she is, I'm thinking. But she hasn't been dragged out of her house today while her mom stands there screaming. I pull my arm back and let it fly, punching Harriet like I'm in a John Wayne movie. I'm expecting her to come back at me full throttle and try to brace myself, but instead she sinks like a stone.

"You killed her!" Judy screams. Harriet lies there, flat on her back. When nobody says anything, Judy screams again.

I'm not sure what happened next, exactly. I think Harriet must have reached out and grabbed my leg because I fall backward and hit my head. The next thing I know Harriet's pulling my hair so hard it's coming out in chunks. I kick her ankle and she lets go, but then her nose starts bleeding and that makes her really mad. She pushes me down and starts slapping me, and then I see Manuela trying to pull her off. When Harriet turns around to punch Manuela, she's stopped by a woman's voice.

"What y'all doin'?" the woman calls. I look up to see a long, thin arm and bright blue eyes in a wrinkly face. The woman looking at me has white hair in curls around her head and sounds like she's from the South.

"I said, what's going on?" the woman says as she pulls Harriet up.

Harriet rubs her nose and sniffles. "She punched me!"

"Who punched you?"

"Her—whatever her name is. The new girl."

"That so?" the woman says, holding out a hand to me. Even though she's old and thin, her arm is strong and she gets me on my feet in half a second. "What *is* your name, new girl?"

"Ruby."

"Ruby, huh? Well, my name is Rose and I have a piece of advice for you. Don't let our director, Mr. Sinningson, catch you fighting."

"She started it!" Harriet says.

Rose leans down to peer at me. "I'm going to give you a break, Ruby, 'cause you just got here. And I know you probably had a hard day."

I look at her without answering.

"But you know if they catch you again, they can send you to juvie. You know what that is?"

"No."

"Juvenile hall," says Harriet, and Rose turns to look at her.

"That's right," says Rose.

"I think she should go there now," Harriet says.

"And I think you should both apologize."

"I didn't start nothin'!" Harriet says.

Rose folds her arms, looking at us both.

"She punched me for no reason," Harriet says.

"Listen, Harriet—" says Rose.

"*Miss* Harriet to you—"

Rose turns to me. "Is that what happened?"

"Shut up, Rose," Harriet tells her. "Or I'll tell Sin what a crumb you are—"

"And then what?" says Rose. "You think he's going to find someone else to take the guff you guys dish out?"

I find myself starting to smile when Harriet glares at me.

"Judy," Rose continues, "what happened?"

"Um, well—Harriet was just trying to be friendly. You know how it is. But, um, Ruby didn't want to talk to us," Judy says, blinking.

"She was pushing Manuela," I say, when Rose shakes her head.

"Okay—all of you. For the last time, you better be nice to each other. 'Cause there's nobody else who's going to be nice to you. Understand?"

Manuela turns away and Judy looks down at the floor.

"Still," Harriet whines. "My nose really hurts."

"All right, *Miss* Harriet," sighs Rose. "Let's take a look."

She leads Harriet toward the door and the other girls follow. At the door, Rose turns around to look at me.

"We're gonna have to find you a pillow, but it may take awhile. I don't know why, but they're in short supply around here. Meanwhile, dinner's in half an hour. You want to come down?"

"No."

"No, what?" Rose asks.

I look at her blankly.

"No, thank you," she prompts me.

"Oh," I say. "No, thank you."

"You won't eat until breakfast if you skip tonight."

"I know."

"All righty, then," Rose sighs. She heads for the stairs and Judy follows, but as soon as Rose leaves, Harriet wheels around and pops Manuela—right in the mouth. I lunge at Harriet but she's too quick for me, shoving my hands away before she rushes out the door.

"You okay?" I ask Manuela.

"Sure," she says, rubbing her mouth. "She is too stupid to hurt me."

"Yeah, well, she hurt me."

"I'm sorry," she says.

"Don't worry about it."

"What about dinner?"

"I don't care."

"Want me to bring it back here? I can put it in my shirt and they won't see."

"I want you to leave me alone," I say, looking out the window.

"*Tú* cannot go without eating," Manuela says.

It takes me a second to figure out that "*tú*" means "you."

"You can if you're on a hunger strike."

"Is that what *tú* are doing?" she says.

I pull on the window, but no matter how hard I tug, it won't budge. Manuela tries to help but she

can't move it either. "I think they paint it shut,"
she says.

"You're kidding."

"The one in the corner opens," says Manuela.
"But we need permission."

"To open a window? You're kidding, right?"

Manuela shrugs.

I lean my head against the pane, shutting my eyes
tight so I won't be able to cry. If I have to stay here
tonight I should at least be able to open a window.

"Sure *tú* are not wanting something?"

"Just for you to go," I say. After a minute I hear
Manuela's shoes on the stairs.

Where is this place? I open my eyes. It's got to be
Brooklyn because we went over the Brooklyn Bridge
and followed a sign that said Jay Street. It's the ugli-
est building on the block, wide and squat, and if it
had a color you wouldn't know it. I think it's yellow,
but it could easily be gray.

I hear Rose joking around in the kitchen while
forks and bowls clatter on the table downstairs. Not
four miles from here, Sophie is feeding her turtle
while her mom, Mrs. Tania, heats up Chinese take-
out on the stove. Les and Bo are eating leftovers from
their party, and I bet the Soroccos are having lasagna.

I've got to stop thinking about food.

Where is Ray? Did he come home or did somebody
warn him? What about Nell-mom? Will she call Gary
Daddy-o and will he have to stop touring? What did

she mean when she said it was all his fault? She hates it when he's on the road a lot, but what else can he do? It isn't fair to blame him for landing me here.

I walk over to the bed by the corner, which has no blankets or pillows on it. If the window opens, I'm sleeping here. I pull up on the window's handle and it moves. Finally! I'm getting somewhere. It smells like a mixture of gas and tar outside but it's better than room air. I pull the window up all the way, letting in a breeze that cools my face.

I lean over the sill, looking down at the street.

I asked Nell-mom about Wisconsin once and she said it was like the rest of the world—regular and real. She said the only place that wasn't real was the place in your head, but that Beats were really good at making that place up and that's why we all got together.

But there are no Beats around here, and I'm stuck in the regular real world. If I don't show up at Blue Skies tomorrow, Sky and Blu will be wondering where I am. Except if no one knows where to find me, how am I going to get home—and what will happen to Solange? She's been with me since I was eight. When we brought her home she was a tiny black ball of fur with a sandpaper tongue. I used to put oil from our tuna can on my fingers and let her lick it off. After a while she'd lick my fingers anyway, whether I had tuna on them or not. Now she sleeps with me every night, and tonight she'll come looking and I won't be there.

She likes to wait at the door until I get out of the bathroom. By that time, Ray's hitting the sack and Nell-mom and Gary Daddy-o are pulling out the foldout couch in the living room. As soon as the bathroom door opens, Solange jumps onto my bed and waits for me, with greeny-yellow eyes wide and her tail standing straight in the air.

I have to make sure my hair is spread out on the pillow so she can sleep on it. First she kneads my hair with her claws like she's making bread or something. Then she goes around and around in a circle for a while and finally plunks herself down, purring. If I get up for any reason, like to get a glass of water, she has to do the whole thing over before she settles down again.

Bang, buzz, clitter-clatter. Noises ricochet upward, making me jump. I can live without seeing my family, even Sophie, Gordy, Sky, and Blu. But how do you live without your cat?

> *I dreamed I was Egypt*
> *The whole Pyramid*
> *With the head of a lion*
> *Like my cat Solange*
> *In a movie in Hollywood . . .*

I'm trying to remember the poem I wrote about her. It was the last poem I wrote before all this started—before I went to bed Friday. It had something about movie stars and dancing and wanting to be like them.

> *I wanted to sing*
> *But I was a Pyramid*
> *In the open Egypt air*
> *Eyeless, speechless tomb*
> *With all these movie stars dancing*
> *around me*
> *And then Solange jumped down from*
> *the window*
> *With a mouth as wide as summer*
> *Yawning like the Goddess she wants to be*

Someone's car screeches to a stop on the street and someone else gets out of another car, screaming. There is no Egypt here. I close my eyes tight and dig my nails into my neck, trying to distract myself. I'm going to have to stop thinking about all this and figure out what I can use instead of a pillow. Because the way things are going, it could be a long, long time before I get one. Even longer before I get to see my own.

11
Organizadora

I'M IN FRONT of Blue Skies when I look down the street and see a man wearing a tunic with some kind of cloth draped over his shoulder. He's turned his back but I can see he has no hair and I know it's Gandhi. I start running and am about to catch up to him when someone grabs me around the wrist and says, "Hold it, little robber girl."

It's Tina, only she's really, really cold. Ice-cold. Someone else is calling my name, and when I turn around I see Gordy in a white lab coat. He's pointing at a chart, trying frantically to show me something. But then Nell-mom walks by, and Gary Daddy-o follows her, but she's totally ignoring him and won't even look his way. I try to call out to her but Gordy is pulling my sleeve and when I tell him to stop he points to the numbers on his chart, saying, "They just don't add up right." And I say, "So what?" But he says, "If the numbers don't add up, you can't go home."

I look at the chart but it seems like gibberish. When I ask Gordy to explain it, he shakes his head and turns away. By that time Nell-mom and Gary Daddy-o have disappeared and I'm alone. I look frantically up and down Charles Street. Then I look up and the sign says Jay Street. And I know I'm lost.

The next thing I know someone's shaking me. I look up to see Manuela.

"Shhh." She puts her finger over my mouth. It's really cold in here, but the window next to my bed is closed, and Judy and Harriet are sound asleep. Manuela motions for me to follow her but when I lean over to reach for my shoes she shakes her head no.

"Only socks," she whispers as I sit up, shivering. I get out of bed and tiptoe behind her into the bathroom. It's almost as big as my bedroom at home, with chipped tile floors and a line of sinks and showers. There's a night-light on so you can see your way around, and I make a beeline for the sink.

I don't know if it's because I haven't eaten in a while but I'm dying of thirst and swallow handfuls of water from the tap for, like, ten minutes straight. This whole fasting thing must be giving me hallucinations because the water tastes incredible—like it's coming from a spring in the mountains instead of a rusty old faucet in a children's home.

Why do they call it a children's home anyway? It's a home for adults with children stuck in it.

There's not a teddy bear in sight, let alone dolls or books or toys or anything you'd want in your house.

By the time I'm done slurping, Manuela is pulling open the shower curtain and pointing toward the drain. Just above it is something that looks like someone drew a square on the side of the wall. Manuela squats down, pushing on it—but nothing happens. Then she looks up at me. "Come."

"What?"

She puts my hand on the square, closing her fingers over mine. Manuela's hand pushes against mine softly and then together, we push at the square. This time it opens, and I can see what looks like a big silver pipe going who knows where.

I look up at her and shake my head. I'm not going into any more tunnels; I've had enough to last me a lifetime. But Manuela is already squeezing herself into the darkness behind the opening and doesn't stop when she sees me shaking my head.

"It's okay," she whispers softly. "Come on."

"What's in there?"

"It is crawl space to the main floor."

"Can't we use the staircase?"

"We do not want Rose to hear. Hurry!"

"But—"

"What is wrong?" Manuela asks.

I want to tell her I'm claustrophobic, but I'm not sure she'd understand—and it feels kind of dumb when she's so cool about all this.

"Ruby," she whispers.

"Yeah," I whisper back.

"Go in feet first and put back to the wall," she says softly. "Use, how you say . . . this foot to feel for the bottom."

I do what Manuela tells me, backing into the square hole, little by little. I can't believe Judy and Harriet haven't woken up by now, but no one's stopping us. "We better not get stuck somewhere," I whisper, knowing Manuela's too far away by now to hear. I lower myself slowly until I feel my toe connecting with something solid. Another inch or two and I'm in.

Whatever I'm standing on doesn't feel very wide. There's a metal bar next to me and I grab hold, trying to see in the near-total darkness.

"Come, Ruby," Manuela says in a normal voice. She takes my hand and we inch forward. "Don't look down. Stay behind me," she cautions. "It is tight."

Great. I don't just get a dark tunnel, I get a narrow one. I can hear the sound of water far below us. "What is that?"

"I don't know," Manuela says. "Maybe sewer."

The bar disappears and I have to walk into the dark without anything to hold on to except Manuela's hand. "Just a little more," she whispers. We walk like crabs, creeping sideways for what seems like forever. I think about rats, spiders, and centipedes behind and around us. On muggy summer nights, the creepy-crawlies come out of our sink and race across the wall and floor. I used to scream when I saw them, and Ray would make fun of me. I'm too old to scream now. But if a rat was by my foot here, what would I do?

Suddenly Manuela lets go of my hand and kneels, stretching her arm out in front of her. A patch of light appears as Manuela pushes open a trapdoor. We crawl into something that appears to be a coat closet, and then Manuela slides out and I follow her onto a rug in front of a bookcase. I can feel myself shivering as I move.

This must be the living room. It looks much nicer than the ones upstairs. There's a chandelier over an upholstered chair and end table, and a sofa that reminds me of the Sheboygan couch pictures.

Manuela raises herself to a sitting position on the rug. "Stay down," she whispers. "And . . . shhh. Like mouse."

"I know," I whisper back. "But you know what I'm thinking?"

Manuela looks at me, hooking her arms around her knees.

"They're all asleep and it's—just you and me."

"So?"

"So why don't we leave, Manuela? Run out and get on the subway."

She smirks. "They have alarm, Ruby. We never make it out of here."

"They're going to have to catch me."

"They will."

"No."

"Well, that is what I like," says Manuela. "*Tú* are brave and not afraid to try things. But there is another way and it comes from what *tú* are telling me. What is this 'hunger strike'?"

I start talking about my conversation with Gregory Corso, but as soon as I say the word *Gandhi*, Manuela sits up. "I know him!" she says aloud.

"Shhh!"

"Excuse me," Manuela whispers. "I am sorry. But I know all about Gandhi because he teaches people . . . *organizadora*—"

"Organ—what?"

"It is a protest so they change people's mind. To bring people together, we must—"

"Organize!" I say, and now it's Manuela's turn to shush me.

"Exactly!" she whispers. "There is a man in our Spanish community—he is like Gandhi for us here in America. His name is Cesar Chavez, and he is trying to help the workers."

"What does he do?" I ask.

"Now, he is just talking and listening," she says, "so he can learn. One day he will lead all of us in a protest. But for now he is just . . . to start."

"Start what?"

"Someday he will lead the people. Chavez tries to help the ones who come from Mexico—"

"Is that where you're from?" I ask.

"I was born there but then we come here. *Mi padre* was in a strike too, not hunger, but at work—so they take him to jail."

"Your *padre*?"

"Papa."

"Okay."

"Mama didn't have enough food for me so they put me here," Manuela says. "She is try to get Papa out of jail."

"What about the other girls? Are they both orphans?"

"Nobody here is orphan," says Manuela. We are all here for . . . trouble. Some kind of trouble at home."

"What about Harriet?"

"She lives with aunt and uncle, but I think they are crazy—"

"That makes sense."

"And Judy's mother has many children and lives with her sister. So they drop her off here for a while."

"How long?"

"Two months, maybe longer. She is two months so far."

So it's not a home. It's a way station.

"And who's that director guy Sinningson? What's he like?"

"He does not come here a lot. But when he does, he can be—how to say. He is rude and unkind. We call him Mr. Sin."

A door creaks upstairs and Manuela grabs my arm. We listen, holding our breath in the darkness. Someone pads out to the landing and then we hear the bathroom door close. My heart is beating so loud, it sounds like a radio, and I know Manuela can hear it.

I count to sixty, then sixty-five. The toilet flushes and Manuela rushes back into the coat closet, pulling me in with her. I try to make myself still, like Yogi does when he meditates. As the sound of water fills the pipes behind the wall, someone upstairs turns on the faucet and the whole wall starts to groan. It's so loud I think the house will fall down.

Manuela takes my hand as we wait, barely breathing. Finally, the sink is turned off and the groaning stops. The door creaks open again and I put my hand to my mouth. Manuela shrinks back as the footsteps grow louder, then stop. If it's Rose, she'll come down, I think, but she doesn't, and after a while her footsteps grow softer and finally fade.

I wipe my face, which is dripping with sweat. Manuela opens the trapdoor, lowering her feet so she can jump in if she has to. She leans in close and whispers in my ear: "So, what *tú* are thinking? Can I join this hunger strike?"

"I don't even know if I can do it."

"Why not?"

"You're asking me that because you haven't tried."

"Papa did it once, and I try with him for a day," Manuela says. "It's hard but I can do it."

"I doubt Judy and Harriet will."

"That is okay."

I rub the spot on my head where Harriet pulled my hair. It's starting to feel sore and I wish I had some ice or something. Ray always says you have to put ice on a bruise within the first twenty-four hours, and I can almost hear him saying it now. But I don't even know where the stupid freezer is.

"Ruby?" Manuela whispers.

I stop rubbing my head; I'm in for a bump no matter what I do. I know Manuela is looking at me, and once I agree to a hunger strike, I'll have to go through with it.

"If we do it, we have to have water," I say.

"Did Gandhi?"

"I don't care," I say. "Without water you die."

"All right, Ruby," says Manuela. "*Tú* are good *organizadora*—"

"If that means organizer, I'm not," I say.

"Still, I think so." Manuela squeezes my hand, and I can tell she thinks it's all settled. But I'm still not sure.

"It will be okay, Ruby," she says, and I look into her eyes, which I can see are shining, even in the dark. I think of how Harriet went after her and how she didn't cry or say anything, even though it must have hurt. She may have been here awhile now and she's looking to me to help her—which is pretty funny, considering how much I need help.

"Manuela—"

"*Tú* are not having to make decision now."

"I'll do it," I hear myself say.

"Oh, Ruby!"

What am I doing? And who does this chick Manuela think I am?

"*Tú* are so good," she says, and for some weird reason, I start to feel excited, like I did when I was talking to Corso at Les and Bo's.

"*De nada,*" I say—the only Spanish words I know. They mean "it's nothing," and as soon as I say them, I wish I hadn't. Because when you think about it, which I don't really want to do—that's what Manuela and I are looking at. A whole lot of nothing—for what could be a long, long time.

12
School

Children's Home Association
2679 Jay Street
Brooklyn, New York

April 8, 1958

42 Bedford Street
New York, N.Y.

Dear Sophie,

I know you're reading this and thinking, where is she? I'm writing you because Nell-mom is probably mad at me and I'm not sure when Gary Daddy-o will be home or if Ray had to leave, too.

There's some stuff I can say and stuff I can't, but the main thing is, I was brought here by a social worker and have to stay by law. My teacher here, Mrs. Brandt, says today is let-ter-writing day, but just so you know, SHE mails the letters.

The main thing I'm worried about is Solange. I'm not sure if anyone's going to take care of her, so can you? Just keep her until I get home is all I ask. Or at least go over and feed her?

I want to get out of here as soon as possible but I can only do that if my mom and dad get married. I think they have to do it in City Hall or someplace like that. So here's what I need you to do: tell YOUR mom to keep bugging N. and G.D-o. They need to get hitched as soon as possible or I'll have to start learning math. And I may never be able to see Solange again. Or you.

Oh, one more thing. There's a guy named Gregory Corso, you know, the poet? He's got a poem of mine in his notebook and hangs out at Chumley's. It's a long story and I'll tell you when I get out. But meanwhile, can you get word to him or someone at Chumley's that I'm here? And while you're at it, you might as well tell Gordy, Sky, Blu, and everyone else we know. They've got to allow visitors and I'd really appreciate it if you'd come.

I have a couple ideas on how to get home but they may not work, so remember to tell Nell-mom and Gary Daddy-o what I told you. It has to be now since my golden birthday will be here REALLY SOON and AS YOU KNOW, whatever you do on your golden birthday is like a preview of the rest of your life (!!!) So I can NOT be here for any reason on that day!

I wouldn't be writing unless it was URGENT.

Love,
Ruby

P.S. If you find Corso, tell him I'm going ahead with that plan we talked about and he needs to tell the papers. He'll know what you mean.

P.P.S. Don't forget Solange—she could STARVE unless you take care of her.

I frown, looking at the letter. Should I tell Sophie what Nell-mom said about getting married? Why did she say they can't? She was probably just upset and didn't mean anything by it. I know most Beats think marriage is kind of old-fashioned, but this is an emergency.

This is all your father's fault. Can't be bothered with us. That isn't true, so why did she say it? I shake my head and put the pencil down. I'm not going to worry about it now. I have enough to worry about.

I fold up the letter and Mrs. Brandt says she'll mail it for me. I can tell she's been reading over my shoulder even though she's pretending not to. But Manuela says it's illegal to tamper with people's letters, so I think they have to send it no matter what.

I was hoping we wouldn't do numbers yet but they want to start on them right away. At Sky's we mostly ran the cash register and I knew times tables and some division. But here they're working on all kinds of things like decimals, fractions, and some really weird shapes like rhombuses and isosceles.

"Manuela?" asks Mrs. Brandt. "Can you tell me what an isosceles triangle is?"

"Okay," Manuela answers. "Two sides of the triangle are equal."

"See, Ruby?" Mrs. Brandt is drawing the triangle on the board as I lean forward to get a look at it.

It seems like Judy, Harriet, and Manuela know exactly what Mrs. Brandt is talking about and I'm the only one who doesn't have a clue what an isosceles is. I feel like I'm back in my dream with Gordy, trying to read numbers on a chart that make no sense. If this is the kind of stuff I'm supposed to know for Levitt's standards test, I'll never pass.

I squint, trying to figure out the spindly chalk numbers on the board. It's even harder to concentrate when you're hungry—let alone starving to death. Mrs. Brandt is talking about measuring angles and plane figures and something else called obtuse angles, but all I can think about is lunch. They had toast and juice for breakfast with scrambled eggs and I had to pinch my hand the whole time I was sitting at the table. Manuela didn't seem to mind nearly as much but she hasn't been at it for two days. She didn't even drink water but I had three glasses—and could have had more.

A right triangle has one right angle. An equilateral triangle has all three sides that are the same. And old isosceles was named for a Greek guy—at least that's what I heard. I don't even know where I heard it but I think it may be true. I'm starting to get really dizzy and it's not even ten o'clock. Plus my head is hurting from yesterday's fight, and there's a good-sized bump starting to swell, just like I thought it would.

"Ruby?"

Mrs. Brandt is calling me and everyone else is staring. I look up.

"Do you want to try drawing some of these triangles?"

I shrug.

"Why don't you try?"

I get up and walk to the board on shaky legs.

Mrs. Brandt hands me a ruler. When I hold it up to the board, she tells me to hold it higher.

As soon as I start drawing the triangle, I can feel my hands quivering. Judy and Harriet start to laugh behind my back.

"Harriet?" Mrs. Brandt says, but I can't hear anymore. I have to put the ruler down because the ground goes soft and wavy and it's all I can do to keep standing.

"Ruby!"

I'm lying on my back and Judy's screaming. I'm starting to get used to those screams, which sound like someone in a horror movie. Mrs. Brandt is calling for help and Manuela is leaning over me.

"Don't worry," she whispers. "It's working."

I close my eyes. Only instead of carrying me upstairs, which is what they should have done, someone throws water at me.

Harriet.

I sit up.

"Thanks."

"Don't mention it, dummy."

"I'm not a dummy."

"You sure seem to be."

"Harriet!" Mrs. Brandt rushes toward us with Rose at her side.

"Leave that child alone," Rose is saying.

Mrs. Brandt helps me to my feet and walks me back to my desk. "What's wrong, Ruby? What's the matter with you?"

"She hasn't eaten since she got here," says Rose.

"Nothing?" asks Mrs. Brandt.

"Not so I've seen."

Mrs. Brandt squats down to look at me. "What are you doing?"

I slide into my seat, looking down at my lap without answering.

"Ruby?"

I look at Manuela, who shakes her head.

"What's going on here? Rose?" Mrs. Brandt asks.

"I don't know, ma'am," says Rose. "They're all upset when they come here."

"Well, she has—you have to eat, Ruby. You can't learn if you don't eat."

She looks like she's expecting me to say something. But I don't.

"All right," Mrs. Brandt sighs. "Do you know what happens to people who stop eating?"

I shake my head.

"You get dizzy and tired—like you are now. But then your body gets cold and won't function properly. Your stomach starts hurting and then bloats up like a balloon. And if you still don't eat, it gets worse. You start losing your reason—and your ability to talk and think. Finally your kidneys go—and believe me I've seen it happen like that. When that happens you can't go to the bathroom normally because you're in what they call renal failure—"

I want to stop listening but she goes on and on.

"Then all the other organs stop functioning and your liver starts to shut down. In fact all of you goes down—like a zombie. All you can do is lie in a hospital bed. Do you really want that?"

I look at her. "No."

"Then why aren't you eating?"

I want to say, "Give me something now!" But Manuela jumps in front of me.

"She is on strike," Manuela says. "We both are."

Mrs. Brandt turns to look at her sharply. "What?"

"A hunger strike."

Mrs. Brandt turns to me again. "Ruby? Is this true?"

"Yeah."

She leans toward me, raising her eyebrows. "What do you mean?"

I want to tell her about Gandhi and Chavez and protesting for my rights. But I'm tired and hungry and I know whatever I say won't sound right, so I look at the floor.

"Ruby?" says Mrs. Brandt. "What do you hope to gain by this?"

"Attention," says Manuela.

"WHAT?"

"People need to know we are here and do not want to be," Manuela continues.

Mrs. Brandt folds her arms. "Do you really think people don't know where you are?" she asks.

"We have the right to be home with our families!"

Mrs. Brandt draws closer to Manuela. "The only thing you have, my dear, is us. And if you don't obey the rules—"

"It's not against the rule to hunger strike," says Manuela. "And if people start to hear about this and it goes into the papers—"

"It's NOT going to get in any paper," says Mrs. Brandt.

"But what if it does?" retorts Manuela.

"Why don't we see what Mrs. Levitt says?" Mrs. Brandt replies.

"I'm not going to eat," I say. It's not much but it's all I can muster.

"Are you nuts?" Harriet calls out, but her voice sounds distant and muffled. "She just said you'll lose your mind!"

"Not to mention your kidneys," Judy says.

She keeps talking but it's getting harder to hear her. I look at Manuela, who's staring at me like I'm her hero or something, which is hard because I'd do anything right now for a piece of toast even if it had no butter. The only thing good about any of this is that it's keeping Mrs. Brandt from her triangles, but that's the *only* thing. At least all this hunger stuff makes you sleepy, and when you're sleepy you don't think about eating.

"Ruby?" Mrs. Brandt says, but when I turn to look at her, Judy screams again—which is how I know I'm hitting the floor.

13
Voices and Visitors

THE CLOSET DOOR is opening and closing, but I can't see anyone. There's a picture of a duck on the opposite wall with a green head and brown feathers, and next to it is a tall glass cabinet with what looks to be medicines inside. I'm guessing this is the infirmary. But the closet door seems to be moving all by itself and gives me the creeps.

Voices are coming from the hall outside but I can't hear what they're saying. After a while they fade away and the closet door opens again. I try to sit up but I'm exhausted. Out of the corner of my eye I see a dark shape walking toward me and then I look up.

"Manuela?"

She puts her finger to my lips and slips something in my mouth. It's dry and wrinkly and makes me want to puke. I try to spit it out but Manuela spreads her hand over my mouth.

"Raisin," she whispers. "Chew."

Is she crazy? I'm supposed to be on a hunger strike.

"Must not get sick, *amiga*. That means friend, yes? Now, eat the raisins and we don't tell them. But hurry—chew."

She puts a few more in my mouth and before I know it I'm eating the most incredible-tasting raisins I've ever had in my life. I used to hate raisins but these are amazing. They must have a chocolate coating or something because they're so tasty and sweet. I'm sucking them in so hard I practically inhale my cheeks, but then we hear footsteps and Manuela pulls away.

"Ruby?" Someone calls my name in the room next door. Manuela shoves a small box into my hand and scampers into the closet. I slip the box under the pillow and close my eyes as the footsteps get closer.

"She's asleep," a deep voice pronounces. Someone kneels next to me.

"Ruby?" It's Rose. I keep my eyes closed and lie there, still as a statue.

A low murmur answers her. I hear the words *bad* and *can't*, and then something about a hospital. It's definitely a man talking, and must be the director, Mr. Sinningson. I try to peek but don't want him to catch me.

"I know, sir," says Rose.

"Don't keep saying 'I know.'"

Rose's dress swishes as she turns, following the man out. Their voices soften in the hallway. I turn around to reach under the pillow and pull out the box of raisins. I'm trying to squeeze my fingers into the box but I can barely get one or two out that way so I rip the box open, swallowing everything except the cardboard, which I have to stop myself from devouring, too.

Manuela pokes her head out of the closet.

"It's okay," I whisper. "They're gone."

"Give me the box."

"Huh?"

"Want them to find it?"

"Oh," I say. "Here."

She pockets it.

"Hey, Manuela. You got any more?"

"Not now," she says. "But I look."

"Well, hurry back, you know? I'm dying here—"

"Raisins will stop the dying," she whispers. "I see what I can do."

"You got water?"

She points at the sink. "See?" I nod.

"Give me a leg up," she says.

"What?"

"I'm going out that way," Manuela says, and I follow her eyes upward to the window. She climbs onto my bed but I'm too weak to give her a boost so she pulls herself up and then whispers, "Psst!" I look up to see Manuela holding up her thumb and smiling like she's in a Robin Hood flick. "Doing good, *amiga*," she says, but slides out the window before I can respond. I hear a couple of thuds and then a tapping sound.

"Manuela?" I call, but there's no answer. I call again. Nothing. About a half minute later I hear a series of taps and lean back against the pillows, staring at the duck on the wall. How is Manuela climbing through windows when I feel like sleeping all the time? Does she have more raisins than I do?

"Ruby?"

The door swings open and I look up to see Harriet, with Judy close at her heels. She strides up to the bed and leans over me.

"You're scaring them silly. You know?" Harriet whispers.

I turn on my side, watching her and Judy. "It's a protest," I say.

"Whatever it is, it's making them crazy," Harriet says.

"Is it hard? Are you hungry?" Judy asks.

"Of course it's hard," Harriet snorts.

"I just want to know," Judy whispers as the door flies open. Rose rushes in, followed by Mrs. Levitt.

"Here she is," she says. "See?"

I turn my head as Levitt pushes past Harriet and Judy. She's wearing perfume today, and a tweed suit with a high collar. The perfume is way too strong, and even though I'm not eating much, it's starting to make me nauseous.

Mrs. Levitt kneels next to the bed. "How are you today, Ruby?"

"Okay."

"You have to eat something. You know that, don't you?"

Harriet pokes Mrs. Levitt. "What's going to happen to her?"

"Don't push, dear."

"If she dies, it's your fault."

"Now, now," says Mrs. Levitt, but I can see her hands are shaking.

"You'll go to jail," Harriet continues.

Mrs. Levitt leans closer to me. "I'm sure Ruby won't let that happen."

The only other time I saw Levitt shaking was in our apartment before she took me away. I remember thinking she really cared about me, and wonder what she's thinking now.

"Ruby, I can't let you go on this way," Levitt continues.

"But you can't stop me either."

"*What?*"

It's not until she answers that I realize I was talking out loud. Levitt's voice is rising now, sounding almost like Nell-mom when she's worried. "I am not going to tolerate this, young lady."

I turn around to face her, and suddenly I'm not nauseous at all. Because I'm not looking at Mrs. Levitt, social worker. I'm looking at someone who wants to be in charge but isn't anymore. Not today.

If she dies . . . you'll go to jail.

I prop myself up on the pillow so I can move closer to her. "You know what?"

"What?" Levitt says.

"I'm not going to eat until I get out of here. And you know what else? You can't make me."

Levitt's mouth twitches until she closes it, hard. "We—we'll see about that, Ruby."

"Sooner or later my parents are going to come here. When they find out what's going on, they're going to go to a lawyer, if they haven't already. And the papers. And if you try to force-feed me, I'm going to fight."

"Ruby—"

"My parents will see the bruises if you hurt me," I say. Those raisins must have superpowers because suddenly I have all this energy. It's like I'm a firecracker and at any second, I'll explode.

"NO one's going to hurt you, Ruby. YOU'RE the one who's hurting yourself." Levitt turns, storming out of the room so quickly the medicines bump against each other in the cabinet.

"Wow!" says Harriet, inching closer.

"Show's over," says Rose. "Go on."

"I'll go when I'm good and ready," Harriet says, making Judy giggle. Harriet stares down at me, hands on her hips. "Good luck, Ruby."

"Good luck," Judy echoes.

"I said *get out of here*!" Rose yells. "Now scoot."

Harriet takes her time leaving, so Judy has to go slowly, too.

Rose looks down at me, frowning. "Now look what you've done."

I'm not sure what she means, exactly, except it feels pretty good for a change.

"They may not be able to make you eat here, but they will in the hospital," Rose says. "You want that?"

I don't answer, and after a minute or two she sighs and walks away. The door shuts behind her and I'm alone. I pull the covers over my head, trying to keep from shivering. Will they really take me to a hospital? Who knows?

Then again, I'd say Levitt looks too nervous to make me do anything. So this hunger stuff must be working—and now Manuela is doing it, too. At least I hope she is, though it seems like she's sneaking some morsels here and there. But that won't put her in the infirmary, and she needs to be. Soon.

A small brown spot on the pillow catches my eye and I stick out my tongue. I fold the raisin into my mouth like an anteater, but instead of gobbling it down I hold it in my mouth. If I don't move, it will stay like that for hours, a hot little pebble of wrinkly-sweet.

14
We Shall Overcome

LIKE CORSO SAYS, this is a cause célèbre, and I think it is whether reporters write about it or not. It's a story for millions of readers, only there aren't many protesters—just me, Manuela, Harriet, and Judy, and none of us has eaten for the past two days. Well, I had a few raisins and saltine crackers, and Manuela and I split an apple at three in the morning—but not so anyone knows. We're all in the infirmary now, with a nurse running around us frantically and the director popping in every few minutes to see how we are.

When Mr. Sinningson and the nurse mentioned the hospital, I said I'd tell the doctors how they treat us here, and then Harriet started jumping up and down getting excited. "We treat you fine," the nurse said, and I asked, "Who are they going to believe? Me or you?" She had no answer for that one.

Meanwhile, Manuela found a book in the library about Gandhi, who laid down in front of zillions of English soldiers running their horses at him. Instead of trampling him and his friends, the soldiers stopped at the last minute because they didn't want the world to think they were nasty even though they were.

"This is how Gandhi did it," says Manuela. "He say when we are violent, it is easy to punish us. When we are protesting in nonviolence, they cannot say we are doing something wrong. What we are doing is protesting with our hunger, because they take us from our families. We do not give up until they let us go home."

I can't say I like this hunger stuff much but I'm starting to see what Manuela means. When you get a lot of people to want the same thing you want, you can make things happen. The thought of this makes me thirsty and I get up to get a drink. I can tell Harriet is watching me as I pull a mug down from the little shelf above the sink and fill it. I turn to Harriet, holding out the mug.

"Want some?"

She shakes her head. I drink the water down and it tastes like raisins. I must have raisins on the brain.

"Why are you still having water?" she asks.

"Because without water you die in three days."

Harriet shrugs. I get the feeling she might have a drink later on, but not so anyone can see. She's got to be tougher than all of us; at least, that's how she sees herself.

I raise the mug to my lips again, holding it high so she won't see me watching her. She looks much younger lying down, like a little kid with her short pixie haircut and nightshirt with rolled-up sleeves. Her shoulders are twice the size of Judy's but her wrists and hands are small, with short, stubby fingers that look almost like a child's. For some reason this makes me feel like I can talk to her, or at least come closer without getting her mad.

I spill the rest of the water out and put the mug back on the shelf. Behind me, someone sighs. I turn around to see Harriet staring at me and take a step forward.

"What?"

"Why did they bring you here?"

"Same reason as you. Lousy parents."

"Yeah?"

"What do you mean 'yeah'?"

"Nothing."

We're silent for a minute but nobody moves and I get back into bed. Judy, who has either been asleep or pretending to be, opens her eyes and looks at us. Manuela sits up in bed. Harriet looks down at her hands and I'm getting the feeling she might start to say something. But all of a sudden, Mr. Sin walks in, going straight to Manuela's bed and looking down at her.

"Your father is being deported," he says. "Do you know what that means?"

Manuela doesn't answer him.

"He's going back to Mexico," Sin says. "So your mother and you will, too."

Manuela turns her face away from him without answering.

"Do you want to go back there?"

Silence.

"Well," he says, "whether you do or not, you will, Manuela. You have your father to thank for it."

No wonder they call him "Sin." He turns away, nearly colliding with the nurse who stumbles past him, shaking a thermometer. She tries to get Harriet to open her mouth but has no luck and settles on Judy.

Mr. Sin watches us awhile but we all ignore him. Meanwhile, Manuela starts to sing. She's singing in Spanish so we can't sing with her. But the chorus goes "*Ai, ai, ai, ai, señor.*" She sings this two or three times and after a while I catch the melody and start to join in. Judy pulls the thermometer out of her mouth, and Harriet starts clapping, which makes Manuela sing louder. The director snorts in disgust and leaves the room, punching the door with his fist.

When Manuela's song finishes, I remember something Sky taught us that's supposed to be a protest song. "We shall over . . . come . . ." I sing softly, holding out the notes to see if Manuela will join in. She doesn't, but in a minute Judy is singing with me. It's the first time I've really heard her (besides the screams), because her voice is so tiny and squeaky, like a mouse. But now she's singing like she's onstage, loud and high and clear as a bell.

"Ohh—oh, deep in my heart," we sing. "I do believe. We shall overcome . . . some day."

Out of the corner of my eye, I see Manuela looking over her shoulder at Rose, who is watching us from the doorway. Judy and I start on the second chorus, and I get a little louder, knowing we have an audience. Rose is as still as a statue, and if I didn't know better I'd almost swear I could see her mouthing the words.

I sit up and then kneel, leaning over Harriet's bed. For some reason I can't explain, I take her hand and continue singing. She turns to me and I think she's going to smile only she doesn't. A big, dark rumble comes out of her instead, like thunder at the beginning of a storm.

"Mmmph," Harriet groans. "Mooov—Maw-eee!" All of a sudden, she's sobbing, with huge gulps shaking her shoulders. "Mawwww—meee! Mawwww-meee! Mawwww-meee!"

Before I can even react, Rose shoos me away and wraps her arms around Harriet, who is shaking like a leaf. Rose rocks her, saying, "All right, all right," over and over again. I lean back onto my pillow as Manuela reaches out to grab my hand. Judy stares at Harriet, holding her hand to her mouth like she's trying to stop herself from crying. Meanwhile, Harriet's sobs grow bigger and more broken-sound-ing until she runs out of breath and slows down.

After a while, Rose pulls a tissue out of her pocket and Harriet blows her nose.

I steal a glance at Manuela, wondering if what Mr. Sin said is really true. What will happen to her family in Mexico? Will it be good or bad? It has to be better than being here and I know she wants to see her parents again. I want it to work out, but the way Mr. Sin made it sound wasn't so hot. Plus, I kind of want her to stay here, mostly for selfish reasons.

Meanwhile, Harriet seems to have stopped crying, and Rose asks her if she wants some water. Harriet nods and Rose gets her a cup, but while Harriet is drinking, Rose walks over to me. She leans over and says, "Now, Ruby. You've got to stop all this. You hear?"

"What?"

"You know they're starving themselves because of what you're doing. You're a bad influence. You understand?"

I look at Rose, and then at Manuela, but before I can answer someone knocks on the infirmary door. The nurse is back with a doctor, who listens to our hearts and looks in our noses and ears. His breath smells like a sour pickle and I have to turn away when he talks. He wants to know how long it's been since I've eaten and I shrug and say I have no clue. His little light shines into my eyes and ears, and then he clicks it off and turns to Manuela.

I close my eyes, trying to sleep. The doctor is fussing with Harriet, who is yelling at him to get his hands off her. *Slap!* I open my eyes to see her smacking away his hand. I close my eyes again, sighing. For some reason the thought of Harriet hitting the doctor seems incredibly funny and it's all I can do to keep myself from laughing.

"What?" Manuela says, and I try not to look at her. I know as soon I do I'll start sputtering, but she's breathing so oddly I turn my head. Only it's not Manuela I see—it's Levitt. She's standing in the corner with someone I don't recognize. And then I do recognize her and sit up so fast I get woozy and have to lie down again.

Levitt is smiling and looking straight at me like I'm her favorite person in the world. The woman next to her is Nell-mom, only she's cut her long hair in a pageboy, just an inch or so longer than her chin. She's wearing a blue shirtdress, the kind you might wear in Wisconsin, but never in Greenwich Village. And there's something else that's weird—really weird. Nell-mom is wearing pearls!

"Hi, Ruby," Levitt is saying, and I find myself staring at her bright red lipstick and small, even teeth. "It looks like your mother is getting married, isn't that nice?"

I can feel my mouth dropping as I stare.

"So you know what that means, right?" Levitt says. "No more hunger striking! Your mom is taking you home."

15
Bleak and Blue

SOMETHING IS ROTTEN in the state of Denmark. That's what Sky says when things don't add up right on the cash register at Blue Skies. He got that saying from a Shakespeare play called *Hamlet* about a Danish prince whose life was in shambles. As I'm watching Nell-mom in her pearls and shirtdress, I'm thinking something's rotten here, too—though I can't exactly put my finger on it.

Nell-mom's in a hurry so I try to say good-bye to the girls as fast as I can. I borrow a pen from Levitt to give Manuela my address and she puts her arms around my neck. "Will be okay," she whispers.

"But—"

"Mexico will be better," she says. "I have experience now as *organizadora*, yes? I will try and be like Cesar—"

"That's enough," says Mrs. Levitt. But it's not enough. Manuela sits up straight, holding up her

thumb like she did the first time she visited the
infirmary and smiling her Robin Hood smile. I lock
my thumb around Manuela's, knowing Judy and
Harriet are staring at us. Even though we're not
friends, I still feel bad that Judy and Harriet have to
stay here. "Keep it up," I tell them. "Keep striking."

"Now, Ruby," Levitt says. "You're going home
because your mother is doing the right thing—not
because of a hunger strike."

"Maybe, maybe not," I say, but Nell-mom puts
her hand on my shoulder and I can tell she's losing
patience.

"You have to eat before you go, Ruby," Levitt continues. "We have some oatmeal in the kitchen here."

"I've got some cheese in my bag," Nell-mom says,
but Levitt isn't taking no for an answer.

"I have to insist," she says, and I can feel Nell-
mom's hand tightening. It's as cold as ice, and I start
getting scared that maybe she'll have a tantrum again.

I let go of Manuela's hand and turn around to
see Nell-mom hurry out of the room. Judy, Harriet,
and Manuela call out their good-byes and I wave,
following Nell-mom down the stairs.

If I look at them now, I'll start bawling. And I can't.

Mrs. Levitt is right behind us and steers me into
the kitchen, where I take a few sips of water. Nell
stands by the door with my suitcase while I spoon
up some oatmeal. It tastes awful but I'm so hungry
I start devouring it and Mrs. Levitt has to tell me to

slow down. When I'm done, I hand the empty bowl to Levitt and she says we can go.

Once we're on the street, Nell flags down a taxi and I climb inside, thinking of a poem by Allen Ginsberg. It was about two people having the same thoughts, bleak and blue and sad-eyed. I don't know why I'm thinking of it but you know how those things are— they just get in your head sometimes. Nell-mom jumps into the cab and tells the driver we're going to Greenwich Village and it starts to hit me: we're going home. It's the first time I've ever been inside a cab and lucky for me, this one's a Checker. I think Levitt gave Nell-mom money for a taxi because she figures I'm tired from all the hunger striking.

From the window, I can see a mom pushing a black baby carriage, with the baby's white sleeves sticking straight up in the air. A pushcart vendor is selling hot dogs to a man in a Panama hat, who's fishing in his pockets for a tip. The cab stops at a light and I realize: Nell-mom is holding my hand.

She has really cool hands, with long, long fingers and a lot of veins, like you might see in a ghost story or something. Usually, there's paint stains on them, too, most often on the tips of her fingers. Today, though, they're clean, with knuckles as round and pink as the baby shrimp at Ivy's Seafood.

I turn to face her and she smiles. There's so many things to say I can't say them fast enough.

"How's Gary Daddy-o? And Ray-boy?"

Nell-mom puts her arm around my shoulders, pulling me into her like she did when I was a little girl. "Fine," she says. "Come here." I try to think how long it's been since we hugged each other. It must have been a long time because I can't remember it.

We cross the Brooklyn Bridge and I remember how Nell-mom said it was painted a color called Rawlins Red. The mineral used to make the paint was from a mine near someplace called Rawlins in Wyoming. I want to ask her about it but it doesn't feel right to move or say anything. So I lean back and watch cars moving over the bridge.

Blu says a man named Washington Roebling built it. His wife had to help him finish because he went too deep in the water and got a disease called the bends that paralyzed him and ruined his eyes. Blu thinks you have to sacrifice sometimes to do great things, and Roebling sacrificed to make this bridge one of the wonders of the world. For some reason, that makes me think about Gandhi and Manuela and her father and Mexico, and I start to get sad again. I think Nell-mom can sense what I'm feeling because she asks, "Are you okay?"

I lick my lips, trying to decide. I feel like the lady in *King Kong* when he picks her up and shakes her while he's walking through the jungle. When he finally puts her down, it must have been strange to be standing on the ground again. But how do I say that?

"I'm . . . fine. Yeah. Okay."

Nell-mom lifts her arm, shifting away from me. When I look up at her, she takes my hand again, bringing her face close to mine.

"Were they mean to you?"

"Not really."

"Tell me," Nell-mom says. I see a muscle twitching in her cheek. "I want to know everything that happened there. Okay?"

"Why?"

"Why do you think, silly?" she says. "Because it happened to me, too."

I look at her, and then it hits me: since we got in the cab she's been trying to blink back tears. I think Nell-mom is imagining that everything that happened to her when she was a kid is the same exact thing that happened to me.

Only we're not the same. And if I tell her, say, everything that happened from day one, will that make her feel better? Did another girl hit Nell in her foster home? Did she have to sleep without a pillow? Did she sneak away to a private place in the middle of the night and make a pact to go on a hunger strike? Did she miss her cat? Now that I think of it, where's mine?

"Wait," I say. "Solange—"

"She's fine," says Nell-mom. "Sophie took her."

"Did she get my letter?"

"Solange?"

"What?"

Nell-mom is looking at me straight on, and all of a sudden we both start to giggle. It's been so long that we had a joke about something—she used to joke with me all the time. Suddenly, I realize how much I missed it.

"Oh, Ruby," says Nell-mom, wiping her eyes. "Did you write a letter to Sophie?"

"Yeah, I did," I say, but I don't want to tell her what I wrote.

"She didn't tell me that," Nell-mom replies. "She just came by and picked up the cat."

"Okay."

"So . . . are you ever going to tell me what happened?"

We're practically touching foreheads now and I draw back a little. I clear my throat but nothing comes out. If I tell Nell-mom what I've been through at the children's home, she'll get upset again and I like her laughing. She'll start remembering stuff I don't want her to remember and the day will be ruined.

I look at my knees. "It was just a place, like those places are. I don't want to talk about it."

"But—"

"I *really, really* don't."

Two, three, four seconds go by. Then slowly, like you would with a sleeping baby, Nell-mom pulls her hand away and sighs. "Okay." And everything that just happened—the hug, joke, laughing—seem to disappear in that sigh. If there was a chance the two of us could be tight like Sophie and her mom, it was fading fast and I didn't see why. Nell-mom and I never talk much about the important stuff; if I'm going to do that, I talk to Gary Daddy-o because he listens more. Why should it matter so much now?

The light changes and the cab starts up again, squeaking as we turn the corner. I try to touch her again but she moves away, leaning toward the driver.

"Take us to Sorocco's."

"Sorocco's?"

I feel the back of my neck tightening. Did Mr. Sorocco tell Nell-mom about the wine bottle?

"Listen—" I start to say, but Nell-mom cuts me off.

"Okay, I have to tell you something," she says, and I clench my fists. "You can't live with me until after the wedding."

"What? Why not?"

"And another thing—"

"When is the wedding?"

"Week from tomorrow," she says.

"Really?"

Nell-mom folds her arms like she's waiting for an argument. "I wasn't going to do it today and tomorrow's your birthday."

My birthday. Is it really my birthday? I must have lost track. But Nell-mom is still talking. "You'll be staying with Sophie this week," she says.

"Cool!" I feel myself blush as she looks at me. What is she thinking now? That I like Sophie better? Maybe I do.

"Where's Ray been?" I ask.

"Les and Bo's. He's been there since you left—"

"You're kidding."

"I told them he was touring with his father—"

So Ray got to be with Les and Bo while I was at the children's home.

"That's not fair—"

"Ruby, don't start with me."

"But—"

"I don't want to hear about it, okay?"

"Fine," I say. "When did Gary Daddy-o get back?"

"Yesterday."

"Did you call him? Did he know they took me?"

"Of course he knew."

"Where are you getting married?"

Nell-mom turns to the driver again. "Pull over."

"At our place?" I ask.

"Let me pay the driver, okay? Hold on."

We pull over to the curb, and Nell-mom hands the driver five dollars, telling him to keep the change. "Come on," she says, and her voice sounds clipped like when she's with Mrs. Levitt.

"Are you mad at me?" I ask.

"Ruby! Come on!"

I try to catch her eye but she opens the door quickly and steps out, shaking the hair from her eyes without looking back. I can tell the driver's impatient, so I get out of the cab as fast as I can. By the time my feet hit the sidewalk, Nell-mom has disappeared.

How did this happen? Fifteen minutes ago we got into a Checker cab holding hands and now she won't even look at me. What did I do? And what's the deal with the Soroccos? They must have told her I broke their stuff and she's been so preoccupied with getting me home she forgot about it until now. I bet anything that's why we're here.

I put down my suitcase, staring at the door. Since this whole thing started, all I wanted was to be back in the Village. Now that I am, I have a stomach full of butterflies. Of course, standing outside of Sorocco's doesn't help, but it's a lot more than that. Let's just say it's a feeling, okay?

Something's rotten in the state of Denmark. And whatever it is—and it could be anything—it has something to do with Nell-mom's weird, housewife-y blue dress.

16
Rotten Unveiled

"RUBY—COME HE-AH!"

Sophie is in her most dramatic outfit: a long velvet skirt with bare patches here and there, a gypsy shawl, and a Billie Holiday gardenia behind her ear. "Look at you!" She kisses me on both cheeks like they do in French movies and then holds my arms, peering at me like a duchess.

The more I try to get away the tighter she clutches me. "Soph," I whisper. "You're squeezing me to pieces."

Sophie relaxes her grip and then, just when I think it's over, I'm surrounded. Blu rushes out, followed by Gordy and Sky, who is holding a small silver box.

"Happy birthday, Ruby." Sky hands me the box and picks up my suitcase. Then Elena and Mr. Sorocco are coming toward me, and I draw in my breath. "Happy birthday, honey," Mr. Sorocco says, holding out his hand. When I take it, he circles my wrist with his thumb and forefinger. "Look what they did to her. Skin and bone. You see that?" He shakes his head at Sky and Blu.

I try to look as pathetic as I can, fluttering my eyes so I seem frail and weak. But when Mr. Sorocco turns away, Sophie whispers, "He's not going to make you pay for anything. Don't worry."

"Really?" I ask.

Sophie cups her hands around my ear and whispers into it. "Elena ran into your mom, who told her what happened to you. When Elena told her parents, they felt really bad and said if you do come back, they wouldn't charge you for the bottle."

"Does my mom know?"

"Not sure," Sophie whispers, and I think, "Why shouldn't Nell-mom know? Everyone else does." That makes me feel almost as woozy as I did the first day of my hunger strike.

"She's really pale," Blu says. "Let's get her inside."

I'm not sure what happened next, or how I got into the restaurant. I think they carried me, because I don't remember walking, but pretty soon there's a bowl of soup in front of me and Nell-mom is at the table, lifting the spoon to my mouth and feeding me like a baby. The soup is some kind of minestrone and I suck up all of it, barely pausing to breathe. As soon as I finish, Elena pours me some more and Mrs. Sorocco comes out of the freezer to ask if "I like."

"Of course she likes it, Ma," Elena tells her. Mrs. Sorocco seems like she's about to go back into the freezer again, but her husband tells her it's time to eat. "Why's she in the freezer so much?" I whisper to Sophie. She tries to ask her mom but all we get is "You'll understand when you're older." Then Blu smiles and mumbles something about "the change" women go through, how it makes them hotter than Hades. I'm about to ask what that means when Ray walks in with Les and Bo. And even though I barely look at my brother most of the time, for some reason I can't stop looking at him and he can't stop looking at me.

He leans over the table and Nell gets up to let him sit down, but I jump all over him instead. I don't even care that everyone's watching us. When he finally does talk, he says the same thing as Nell-mom: "You okay?"

"Yeah," I say. "Hungry."

This seems to make everybody laugh until Ray looks over at Mr. Sorocco, and says, "Not funny." Then everyone gets quiet again. It's just that way with me and Ray. I get mad at him when he's not around because he always seems to avoid the cruddy stuff, while I seem to run right smack into it. But when we're together he always does something that makes me like him again—like knowing that a hunger strike's no joke.

"Where's Jo-Jo?" Nell-mom asks, changing the subject like she always does when she thinks something might be upsetting my brother. I have to give it to her—she's always been cross-eyed crazy about Ray. I don't really care because I think that's how Gary Daddy-o is about me. But it's funny to see how protective Nell-mom can be with the Ray-boy.

"Jo-Jo's out with friends tonight," he says. Jo-Jo is Ray's girlfriend and does her best to make sure we all know it. She's Chinese and can recite the Pledge of Allegiance backward. For some reason, everyone thinks this is a big deal.

"Okay," Nell-mom says as my brother shrugs. "Did you have a fight?"

"No," Ray says, and I have to stop myself from turning to Sophie and rolling my eyes.

"Well, it's odd she wouldn't come for Ruby's birthday dinner. Don't you think?" Nell-mom asks. What is *wrong* with her? What do I care whether Jo-Jo's here or not?

"Where is Gary Daddy-o?" I ask. Isn't that more important?

Nell-mom looks at Ray but he's looking at Sky, who's looking at me until I catch him at it. I turn to Ray again.

"When's he coming?" I say.

"HERE VE GO!" Mrs. Sorocco sweeps into the room with a huge tray of lasagna. "You eat now, see Daddy later." She sets it down right in front of me and if I wasn't in a roomful of people I'd want to dive into it headfirst, like you do in a swimming pool. There's garlic bread, sausage, fancy mashed potatoes, and something called antipasto, which is a sort of appetizer with olives, pepperoni, and cheese. I haven't seen this much food in—have I ever seen this much? Just for me?

"It doesn't get any better than this," Bo says, but I'm chowing down too fast to answer and it seems like everyone else is, too. Then Gordy shoots his napkin at me in the shape of an airplane. "Come up for air!"

We all laugh, including me.

"Hey," Gordy says. "You know that test you're supposed to take?"

"Shhh. You want to ruin her birthday?" Sophie scowls.

"Well, we have to take it, too," Gordy says.

"Oh, really?"

"Yeah, that social worker says so."

"I was hoping she wouldn't find out about you."

"Well, she did," says Sophie. "And I don't think I'm going to pass."

"You can probably do the English part," I say, but Sophie shakes her head.

"I can maybe do the math," Gordy says.

I've never seen a number Gordy doesn't like, so it's weird to hear him say maybe.

"You guys do what you can," Sky tells him. "Worst that can happen is you go to school."

Gordy nods and in a minute, the table starts moving. I know it's because he's shaking his knee up and down, which is what he does whenever he's nervous. Sophie once said she was glad we weren't in a real school because Gordy's so thin and smart, he'd get a lot of teasing. He's also short, which can't be good in a schoolyard full of bullies.

I look down at my plate, pushing some lasagna onto the bread. I'm starting to feel guilty all over again, since no one would be taking this test if I hadn't messed up at the fruit store.

"Hey, Ruby," says Sophie. "Open your presents." She picks up the silver box from Sky.

I peel back the wrapping slowly and when I open the box, Nell-mom gasps and I nearly fall over. Two gold hoopy earrings, as big as the moon, lie on the white cotton inside the box.

"Put them on, Ruby!" Sophie calls out, and Nell-mom pushes back my hair and helps me fit them into my ears. Then Ray gives me a new notebook, and Sophie and Gordy give me their present, which is almost as good as the earrings—a new leotard, and it's red. Not bright red, more like a burgundy, which isn't the one I was saving for. But now that I see it up close, I like it better—and Nell-mom says it will really set off my hair.

"Can I try it on?" I ask her.

"Why don't you wait till we finish with the presents?" she says. I get a jar of candy from Elena and then I open Nell-mom's present. It's three kinds of nail polish—black, orange, and a burgundy that matches the leotard.

"Hey, thank you," I say, and she smiles. I think maybe she's getting over whatever bugged her in the cab. I look straight at her, smiling back.

"From me you get a free ride," says Mr. Sorocco while his wife says, "Shush!" and frowns.

"What?" he says. "That's a good present. She don't have to work."

"Angelo!" says Mrs. Sorocco, shooing him into the kitchen while Elena tries not to laugh.

"I can polish your nails if you want," Elena says.

"Okay." I push away my plate. It seems like the perfect birthday but Gary Daddy-o's still not here.

"Are you sure he got back from Philly?" I ask Nell-mom.

"Who?"

"What do you mean who? Gary Daddy-o."

Nell-mom starts combing her hair with her hands, and I can see little beads of sweat on her forehead and neck. The room goes quiet except for Sky, who is clearing his throat.

"Nell-mom?"

She looks so weird I turn to Sophie. "Is something wrong?"

"I'm not . . . sure," she says, and then I get that butterfly feeling in my stomach—again.

"Where's my dad?" I say. "Where is he?"

Nell-mom finally looks at me. "Ruby. Listen."

I wait, but she doesn't say any more.

"What's going on?"

"He was in Philadelphia—"

"Is he okay? WHERE IS HE?"

"I just—" Nell-mom stops, looking at Sophie's mother.

"Will someone TELL me what's going on?"

"Come outside with me, Ruby—"

"I don't want to come outside."

"Come out and I'll tell you—"

"I thought you're getting married."

"I am."

"So what are you waiting for, the moon?"

"Ruby. Don't be fresh with me." I look around the room, bewildered. Everyone's staring straight ahead or at the floor.

"Where is Gary Daddy-o? Why isn't he here?" I try to keep my voice from shaking but I can't.

"He's at home."

"Is he mad at me?"

"No, of course not."

"Then—"

"I have to get married, Ruby," says Nell-mom.

"I know," I say. "But I don't understand." Are we both going crazy?

Nell-mom starts twisting her hair and then stops.

"So," she says.

"So, you are getting married. Right?"

"Right," Nell-mom says. "Just not to . . . well . . . your dad."

17
Daddy-o's Here

OUT OF SOROCCO'S, past the laundry, past all the cafés and bars and stores and guys in black T-shirts trying to get girls to look at them; past an accordion player on a unicycle, three jugglers with tennis balls, and the music store with the tenor saxophone in the window Ray would kill for. I don't stop running until I see the awning at 96 Perry and hit the door. It's locked and I left my key here when Levitt took me to the children's home.

I ring the bell for what seems like forever. When no one answers, I start ringing all the bells until someone buzzes me inside. Our apartment is on the first floor behind the stairwell and I have to push away three empty boxes to get to the door.

"GARY DADDY-O," I call.

I hit the door as hard as I can but he won't open it. Is he even home? There are no lights on inside. I sink down, leaning against the door as I lower myself to the floor. I'll sit here until doomsday if I have to. I'm about to start banging again when the door opens. I turn to look up but Gary Daddy-o is already moving backward into the apartment. He doesn't even say hello.

"Dad—Gary Daddy-o?" I walk into the dark hall, which feels hot and stuffy. "Daddy, I'm sorry. Where are you?"

He doesn't answer me. Someone else is coming inside the apartment; it's Ray, who must have followed me. He almost tiptoes, like he's walking on eggs. It's very quiet in here. In fact, it's the quietest I've ever heard. Gary Daddy-o is standing at the living room window, looking out at the street. He hasn't shaved in days and it doesn't seem like he's sleeping much. We stand there for a minute, watching each other.

"Gary Daddy-o?" I say. "It's my birthday tomorrow."

He doesn't answer so I try again.

"Do you hear me? I'll be twelve. On April twelfth. Know what that means?"

"Happy birthday." His voice sounds old.

There's a bottle of Jim Beam on the windowsill.

"When did you get back from Philly?"

"Yes-day."

"What?"

"Day ago."

He picks up the bottle of Jim Beam and drinks. It's a long drink, more of a chug, really. Then he finally puts it down.

"Nell-mom says she called you—"

"She did."

"So didn't you ask—"

"Ruby." Ray is tugging at my arm. "He's not gonna talk."

"Not to you maybe. He'll talk to me."

"I've been trying—" says Ray.

"Gary Daddy-o!" I take his hand but the fingers are cold and damp. He reaches for the bottle again but I grab it first.

"Ruby—"

"No."

"Gimme that—"

"Not until you tell me what's going on."

"Nothin'."

"What?"

"I just said, there is nothin' goin' on." Gary Daddy-o moves away from the window to sit on the couch. The cream-colored shawl falls onto his shoulder, but he doesn't touch it or even seem to notice.

"She called me in Philly," Gary Daddy-o says.

"Said we had to get married right away. I asked if we could talk about it when I got home. Couldn't hear in the hotel room."

"That's not exactly right," says Nell-mom. We must have left the door open because I didn't hear her come in.

"Why don't you tell them what really happened?" she says.

He shakes his head. "Babe—"

"He was in a hotel room with some chippie," Nell-mom says. "He could barely talk—"

"Hey." Gary Daddy-o looks up.

"Says, 'Babe, can't you take care of it?' And I said we have to get married right away. But he hung up on me. Or someone else did."

"I wasn't with anyone—" Gary Daddy-o says.

"Oh, please."

"You're WRONG." His voice rises.

"You *are* wrong!" I repeat. "You shouldn't be saying that."

"It's none of your business, Ruby!" Nell-mom yells. "It's just not."

"It is too—"

"Ruby," says Ray. "Can you let her talk?"

I wheel around to face him. "Don't tell me what to do."

"I'm not."

"You got off scot-free."

"Look," says Ray. "Nell-mom found me at Blue Skies and said to stay at Les and Bo's for a while. She told Levitt I was touring with my dad."

"I know, I heard," I say, setting the bottle of Jim Beam on the coffee table. "But if Nell-mom isn't getting married to Gary Daddy-o, then who?"

"Chaz," says Gary Daddy-o.

I look at Nell-mom. "You mean the guy who owns the gallery on Charles Street? The one you were painting when I came over with the social worker?"

As soon as I say this, Gary Daddy-o fixes his eyes on Nell-mom. That's how I know it's true.

I glare at her. "That guy is *old*. Stupid. And disgusting."

"Ruby—"

"Don't tell me you want to be with Chaz. You love Gary Daddy-o!"

"He's the one who's married," says Nell-mom. "Not me."

"What? What are you talking about?"

"You want to tell her?" says Nell-mom. Gary Daddy-o picks up the bottle again and chugs.

"Tell me what?"

No one says anything.

"WHAT?" I say again.

"Your dad was married a long time ago," says Nell-mom. "He got someone pregnant in high school and had to marry her."

I look at Ray, who is looking at the floor. "What's going on?" I say. "Did you know this?"

"They lost the baby and split up but never divorced," Nell-mom says. "Your dad said he never wanted to do that again—"

"I said I never wanted to make that mistake again," Gary Daddy-o says.

"I'm NOT a mistake," says Nell-mom. "And neither are your children."

"I didn't say that—"

"Now you know, Ruby. Okay?" Nell-mom's face is getting blotchy like it usually does when she's

angry. Watching her now makes me think of the day
Levitt came to our apartment.

This is your father's fault. All of it!

So she's been angry for a while.

"Wait—" I say. But Nell-mom is already walking
out the door.

I turn to Gary Daddy-o. "You can't let her go
like that."

"We have no choice," says Ray.

"Are you kidding?"

"Ruby—"

"WHAT'S THE MATTER WITH YOU?" I know
I'm screaming but can't help it.

Ray gets up and walks into the kitchen. He hates
fighting as much as Gary Daddy-o, but I'm not letting him off the hook.

"You're just going to let her do this to us?"

"She's doing it *for* us, not *to* us," Ray says. He
leans over the sink with his back to me and turns
on the water.

"Is that what you think?"

Ray puts his finger in the water, not answering.
I look down at the sink and realize it's the cleanest
I've ever seen it—no dishes, cups, forks, or saucers.
In fact the whole apartment is clean, or at least, the
clutter's gone. But where is it?

I dash into the living room again and reach for a
lamp, but it's not there. Neither is the table it sits on,
or the clock or bookshelf. I turn on the closet light
to see what's left in here. All I see are the couch and

coffee table and a few cockroaches scurrying under the wall.

I go back to the kitchen. At least the breakfast table and chairs are still here. Ray is still playing with the tap water with his back to me. I go back to my room, pushing the door open. The bed and dresser are gone! I jump into Ray's room and see his bed. What gives?

"Ray!" I run to the kitchen. "My bed is gone."

"Yeah."

"But yours isn't."

He shuts off the water.

"What—"

"Chaz has an extra bed for me."

"I want mine back."

"It's at Chaz's place," Ray says.

"This is *my* place."

"Ruby—"

"NO!"

I rush back to the living room, where Gary Daddy-o is still on the couch with his bottle of whiskey. By now it's almost empty, like his eyes. I kneel down next to him.

"Gary Daddy-o?" I put my hand on his knee but the only thing he looks at is that bottle. I start to wonder if he has another one. He probably does. If not, he knows where to get it.

How long is a minute? How long is it when you're kneeling next to someone who won't look your way?

"Ruby." Ray is calling me from the doorway.

"Go," I tell him.

"We're supposed to be at Sophie's."

"I'll catch up."

Ray stands there staring, and I think, no matter where I go I'll never leave this apartment.

This is forever. This will always be where I live.

I don't want to get up but my knees are starting to hurt so I change positions, sitting cross-legged on the floor. A truck passes by outside, shaking the floorboards. Gary Daddy-o still isn't looking at me but he at least lets me hold his hand. And when I use it to wipe the tear coming down my face, he squeezes my finger, and for a second I think he's going to sob. Instead he grabs me and pulls me onto his lap, which pretty much ends any chance I have of not crying. Then Ray comes over and hugs us both.

"You can't do this," I hear myself say through jagged breaths. "You can't give up on us."

"Ruby," is all he'll say.

"You need to find that lady and divorce her."

"No time," says Gary Daddy-o.

"We'll wait for you. We'll stay at Sophie's."

"Your mom wants to marry someone else now."

"No she doesn't—"

"She does, Ruby. Now let it go."

But I can't let it go.

"Was she right?" I ask. "Was there someone in your hotel room?"

"Honey—"

"Was there?" Gary Daddy-o pulls his arm away. "There's always people around when you go on tour."

"What does that mean?"

"They hang out with us. It's nothing."

He reaches for the bottle but this time, I snatch it and run to the window.

"What are you doing?" Gary Daddy-o says.

I open the window and pour the whiskey out.

"You don't need any more," I say, turning to face him as I set the bottle down.

Gary Daddy-o watches me, but makes no move to get up. I know he can get another bottle, but I'm not going to make it easy for him. He frowns, looking down at his hands. He won't look at either of us, and when Ray tries to touch him, Gary Daddy-o shakes him off. Ray's face darkens and he springs up, heading for the bathroom. I hear the toilet flushing down the hall and remember how Levitt stared at the tub and the cracks in the ceiling, deciding everything was wrong in here. Now it really *is* wrong and it's all her fault.

But it's Gary Daddy-o's fault, too, if there was someone in his hotel room. If he was away all the time, and Nell-mom couldn't count on him. If he was married to someone else—

"Gary Daddy-o, I need you to talk to me."

"You better go, honey," he mumbles.

"I live here. Remember?"

"You can't anymore. You can visit."

"What do you mean 'visit'?"

"Weekends. When I'm around—"

"What do you mean 'around'? Where are you going?"

He doesn't answer and I sit on the windowsill watching him until Ray comes out of the bathroom. "Ruby!" he calls. "We gotta go."

"I'm staying here," I say.

"Nell-mom says we can't do anything to make them send you back—"

"I don't care what Nell-mom says."

Ray comes over and touches Gary Daddy-o's arm. "I love you," he says, and though I don't look up I can hear his voice breaking.

"Love you," Gary Daddy-o says.

Ray closes the door so softly I'm not even sure he's gone.

There is no clock, so I can't tell what time it is. It was starting to get dark when I ran over here, so I'm guessing it's nine or later. I doubt Gary Daddy-o will tell me anything about his life on the road or whatever else he's been through. And do I really want to know?

I sit on the couch and press my head against his cheek, smelling sweat in the creases of his neck. Since he hasn't shaved in a while, his beard is rough and grizzly. After a minute he puts his arm around me and we just stay like that, holding each other.

And even though I don't want to, I can't help but wonder if this could be one of the last times I see him. Because if he keeps going on the road to play his gigs, he could go forever. If he's sad enough.

I won't let him leave us. I can't.

Outside, the street starts to rumble with the sounds of Friday night. A cornet plays in the distance; a group of girls runs by, screaming; a fire-truck siren blasts as it rounds the corner. Other sounds come and go, playing around and through the apartment like an accordion; in, out, over, down.

If I can just hold him like I'm doing now, he can't go anywhere. I tighten my grip around his neck and he lifts his chin so I can lean on his shoulder. That's all I really need anyway—just me and my Gary Daddy-o, watching shadows from the streetlights splash their patterns on the wall.

18
Chaz

I WAKE UP in Ray's bed; Gary Daddy-o must have put me there. There's a note taped to the wall.

Had to go uptown to rehearsal. Your mom wants to see you today and Solange is waiting at Sophie's. B-Good.

—Love, G. Daddy-o

Someone's ringing the buzzer, so I stick my head outside the window to see who it is. Sophie's outside, holding a box that seems to be moving. Solange! I run to the door to buzz her in.

"I thought you might want to see her," Sophie says. She pulls off the top of the box and Solange jumps out, looking ten times bigger than when I left her.

"What have you been feeding this cat?"

"Everything," says Sophie, yawning. "She eats like a horse." I pick up Solange and try to cradle her but she's always been squirmy. She scratches her hind legs against me and jumps down to smell and taste whatever's left in this apartment. I click my tongue at her to see if she'll come, but no luck. I just have to wait until she's ready.

"Want some breakfast?" Sophie asks.

"I don't think there's much in the fridge except beer."

"We've got strawberries and sour-cream omelets at our house," Sophie says. "Wanna come?"

"Nah."

"Come on, Ruby—"

"My mother's there, isn't she?"

"She wants to take you out for your birthday."

"Yeah, well," I say. "I'm out already."

Sophie sits on the floor and calls Solange, who kind of annoys me by coming to her. The cat turns around a few times in a circle before settling on Sophie's lap. I look at her.

"Give her a few days," Sophie says. "She just got used to me."

"You think she's really going to live with Chaz?" I ask.

"Solange?" Sophie scratches her behind the ear.

"Nell-mom."

"Oh. Guess so. He lives over the gallery," Sophie says. "He's got a really big pad."

"Charles on Charles Street," I say, and we both start to laugh. I put my fingers in front of Solange's nose and she sniffs them. After a few minutes of this she lets me scratch her under the chin.

"So is Charles his real name?" Sophie asks, but I shrug. I don't want to talk about Chaz or Charles Street. I'm staying on Perry.

"He bought you a present," Sophie says.

"You can have it."

"It's a leotard."

"What color?"

"Black."

I pet Solange, trying to decide if there's a way to accept something you want from someone you hate. If I keep the leotard at Sophie's I can borrow but not own it.

"They did your room over there."

"I have a great room here," I say.

"They said you can have both rooms," Sophie says.

"I don't give a hoot WHAT they said."

Solange jumps up and runs down the hall and I bring my knees up to my chest. Chaz is rich because a lot of people go to his gallery and buy things. Was he romancing Nell-mom the day we found them in the studio? If that's true, then he's the opposite of cool.

"Can I still go to the bathroom here?" Sophie asks.

"Of course you can go to the bathroom. Why wouldn't you?"

"I don't know." She gets up and walks down the hall, and as I watch her I see why she asked me. The sound of her feet on the floor is really loud, like there's no one around for miles. It's like a ghost house.

"We have to get some food in here," I say to no one.

When Sophie comes out of the bathroom, she leans against the door and calls out, "What are we going to do about school?"

"I don't know." I get up and walk over to her. "I'm betting Gordy will pass the test, but you and I might have to go."

"That would be terrible—"

"There are worse things," I say, "than school."

"Okay, but—"

"I don't care right now, Sophie. I just don't care."

Rat-tat-tat. Nell-mom is knocking on the window. She's standing outside with Chaz, who's wearing a blue shirt with short sleeves and a collar. He looks really square. Nell-mom, on the other hand, looks better than she did yesterday, in a black skirt and boots with her hair swept up in a beret.

"Ruby!"

I don't answer so Nell-mom uses her key to get in. Solange comes back and rubs against her ankles.

"Hey," she says. "You remember Chaz."

I turn my back.

"Ruby!"

"It's okay," says Chaz. "She doesn't have to—"

"Yes, she does," says Nell-mom. "She has to be nice to you."

Sophie backs into my room, closing the door behind her.

"We want to show you the new apartment," Nell says.

"It may be *your* new apartment," I say. "I live *here*."

"Honey, it's okay," says Chaz, and I really hate how he calls her honey. "She can live here for a while—"

"Ruby cannot live here. She can either live with her married mother and stepfather or at a children's home."

"But she can visit her dad."

"Visit means once or twice a week," says Nell-mom. "It does not mean living here."

I turn to face her. "I'd rather go back to the children's home."

"You are going to live with me, Ruby," says Nell-mom. The veins on her neck stand out from her skin like pale blue twigs on a paper napkin.

"Babe—" says Chaz.

"DON'T CALL ME BABE!" Nell-mom yells, and Chaz is quiet. Finally.

I smile. Just give it a few weeks, buddy, and see how *you* like being bossed around.

"Ruby, listen to me." Nell-mom takes hold of my chin and lifts it so I have to look at her. "Mrs. Levitt told me you were starving yourself. She said you were going to die if I didn't do something."

"You don't have to be scared of Mrs. Levitt—"

"But I *do*, Ruby! I do." Nell-mom squats down on the floor in front of me. "She can do anything she wants and we don't have a say in it. You don't know because it never happened to you."

"It did happen—"

"No, Ruby. I didn't let it happen. I'm getting married and we'll be safe—"

"I don't care about being safe. I want my father."

"And you have him," says Nell-mom.

"Not like before."

"We've been through this, Ruby."

"But he'll get divorced, okay? Let him find that lady—"

"It's not just the lady, Ruby! It's your dad and me." Nell-mom puts her hands on my shoulders. "We're better off this way."

I look at her, trying to figure out what could have happened.

"It's not like it was, you know?" she says as though she could read my mind. "We're not the same as we used to be. It isn't your fault."

"Then why can't I live with him? I want to live here at least part of the time."

"You can, sometimes."

"More than sometimes."

"We'll see, okay? We'll see when he's here."

"The more *I'm* here, the more he will be."

"We'll talk about it later, okay?" Nell-mom stands up, brushing off her skirt.

I don't answer.

"Okay, Ruby?"

I stare at Chaz's shoes, knowing they're both watching me. If I push too hard, Nell-mom will dig in her heels and then I'll never get my way. I look up at her. "Okay."

She nods and smiles. "Ready for your birthday breakfast?"

"In a minute."

"Good. We'll see you outside."

Chaz opens the door for Nell-mom and in a few seconds I see them through the window, with their arms around each other. Sophie opens my bedroom door and pokes her head out.

"You okay?"

Sure, just my life is falling apart. But it's not like I can go on another hunger strike right now. I mean, I could but I don't think that would change things. It might make them worse, especially if I got sick or something. The only choice I have is to wait and see what happens.

Or is it?

Let's say for now, I take Solange and go back to Sophie's. I eat breakfast and see my new room. But I'm also going to be scouting out furniture and bringing it back here, because it's not up to Nell-mom and Gary Daddy-o to say where I live anymore.

It's my choice, and my place. No matter what they say or do.

19
Fake Day

THIS IS NOT my golden birthday. It's somebody else's, someone in New Jersey, maybe, or Idaho. This is just a regular day where I get some cupcakes and an omelet made with strawberries and sour cream. There's also a subway ride to Chelsea, where there's a street fair on West Twenty-Sixth because Nell-mom asked me where I wanted to go and I said nowhere. She said let's go to a museum and I said I didn't want to see any art, so Mrs. Tania suggested the street fair.

Sophie's trying hard to make it fun, but it isn't. It could have been if we were by ourselves, but instead we have Chaz trailing along with Nell-mom, Ray, and Mrs. Tania. We go up and down the street looking at food and tables full of books, clothes, toys, and records. Chaz is buying all these little things for Nell-mom, and she's acting all goosey about them and all I can think of is Gary Daddy-o staring out the window with his bottle of Jim Beam. So when Chaz offers to buy me anything I want, I say no and ask if we can leave soon. Then Ray chimes in.

"Come on," he says.

"Leave me alone."

"You always think it's her fault."

I start walking away, but he catches up to me. "She was terrified the whole time you were gone—"

"That doesn't mean she has to marry some jerk—"

"He's not that bad," Ray says, and I look at him like he's crazy.

"Oh, really?"

"You know—"

"You're telling me you like Chaz?"

"I like it when she's happy—"

"You knew this was going to happen," I say. "You knew it that day in the studio."

"I didn't know ANYTHING!" Ray says.

"You're telling me you don't care if you don't see your dad—"

"We'll see him, Ruby! We're both going to see him. For one thing, we'll be out on the road."

"What?"

"He says I can go out on the road with him."

I can't believe what I'm hearing. "You mean . . . on gigs?"

"Not all the time, but sometimes—"

"THAT'S why you don't care," I say. "Because you won't be here."

"You can go, too—"

"How, Ray? I don't sing and I don't play an instrument. What do I do, out on the road?" I try to keep my chin steady but I know it's starting to shake.

"We'll think of something!"

"You're leaving me—"

"I'm not leaving, Ruby, okay? I would never just leave you. Once in a while, for a short gig, maybe—"

I cut him off before he can say any more. "Go AWAY, Ray. Go wherever you want to go. Just don't tell me how to feel when nothing's changing for you."

He tries to grab my arm but I kick him right in the shin and he yowls and lets go. At that point Nell-mom starts walking over to us and it's all I can do to keep from screaming.

"What's the matter?" Nell-mom asks.

"Tell me you really love this guy—"

"He's a good man—"

"And you love him—"

"And I love him, Ruby, yes!"

"Like you love Gary Daddy-o?"

"They're different people. And I love them differently," Nell-mom says, and I can tell she's trying not to cry. "What you don't see is how much I love *you*, Ruby. You refuse to see—"

"Then you're doing this for me—"

"For you and me."

"I don't believe you."

"Fine. Right. Then don't." Nell-mom's eyes go cold and flat, and she's about to turn away when Mrs. Tania waltzes over, all cheery and chirrupy. She says she wants to see where Chaz lives and suddenly Nell-mom perks up and says that's a good idea, I can see my new room and all. A few minutes later, we're on the subway and then on Charles Street, and Chaz is leading us into my room.

It's much bigger than my bedroom at home, and Ray says he'll take the small one. "Is that because you won't be around?" I ask, but he ignores me.

Nell-mom says even though all the rooms are white right now, we can do mine in black if I want. The kitchen has a tile floor, and the rugs are thick like they are at Les and Bo's. But since Chaz doesn't know how to decorate like they do, it's boring except for the pictures, which come from the gallery. But I don't care what color they paint my room. I'm going to hate it no matter what they do.

On the way back to Sophie's, we stop for pizza and as soon as we get there I go to her room and sit on the bed, leaning back against the wall. Sophie follows me and sits down on the rug. Neither one of us wants to say much because we both know what's going on. I'm not going to pretend I'm having a great birthday when it's the worst one I've ever had.

Ray comes to the door to see if I want to talk, but I don't say anything. He says he's going out to meet Jo-Jo and we can talk later, but I don't answer and pretty soon, he goes away. Mrs. Tania, Chaz, and Nell-mom are yakking in the living room and after a while, I hear their glasses clinking, so I guess they're pouring wine.

"Want to play something?" Sophie says. She likes card games and normally I'd say yes, but I'm not in the mood.

"No, thanks."

"Wanna go out?"

"I don't know. Where could we go?"

"There's got to be a reading somewhere. Don't you think?"

"Sophie!" I shoot up from the bed like a rocket.

"Yeah?"

Today's the day—or night, really. "There's a reading at Chumley's—"

"Huh?" Now Sophie is up, too.

"It won't start until nine or ten—"

"We can't get in there! We need a parent or something—"

"No, we don't."

"Ruby, I'm telling you. They don't let kids in there."

I lie back down again. Mrs. Tania might go for it, but there's no way Nell-mom would take me in a million trillion years. But if we get to Sophie's mom first, we might have a chance.

"Ask your mother," I say to Sophie.

"You think?"

"Just ask her without talking to my mom and see what she says."

Sophie leaves the room and I lie on the bed, looking up at the chips and spots on her painted ceiling. She's taped a picture up there of Lucille Ball, who is Sophie's favorite actress. I think Sophie could be like Lucy when she gets older— even funnier. She comes back in the room and I look up at her.

"They won't take us."

"Why not?"

"They're tired—"

"Oh, right." Adults are always tired except when *they* want to go somewhere.

"They said we did a lot today."

"They did a lot, you mean."

"And they'll take us to a reading another time."

"Yeah, great," I say, sitting up so I can see Sophie, who is perched on a floor cushion in a yoga position with her eyes closed.

"What are you doing?" I ask.

"Meditating."

"What for?"

"I need to get to a better space in my head," she says. "Right now I'm just angry. I'm in the here and now, and I need to get out of it."

"Listen, Sophie—"

"Shhh!" Her hands are down by her sides and her legs are crossed, one over the other. The laughter in the other room rises and then flattens like a note in the wrong key. I stare at Sophie's closed eyes behind her glasses and think of Manuela. What would she do if she was me?

They'll stop drinking eventually and have to go to sleep, and when they do I'm out of here. I pull Sophie's curtain back and look out the window. She's on the fourth floor but luckily she has a fire escape. I open the window and Sophie looks up.

"Hey!"

"I thought you were meditating."

"You can't go out there."

"Why not?"

"They'll hear you."

"They have to knock off sometime. Right?"

"Well . . . eventually."

"Right. That's what I mean."

"Oh," Sophie says.

"I promise I'll get us in. You up for it?"

"I guess so."

"Come on, Soph. It's an adventure."

"Okay," she says, looking up at me. "Sure."

There's nothing left at this point but to let the adults get tired. We play three games of War, and Sophie wins all of them. Then she yawns and says we should take a nap.

"How do we wake up in time?" I ask, wishing for once I knew a Beat with an alarm clock.

Sophie yawns again. "It's going to be hours."

"Okay, look," I say. "You go to sleep for a while and I'll hang out by myself here. Then I'll wake you up and we'll go, okay?"

"Okay," she says, and we trade places so she's on the bed and I'm on the floor cushion. I look around for something to read but all Sophie has are fan magazines about actresses and a book about traveling in Paris. Then I see a dictionary. I wanted to look something up before all this happened, but what was it?

Kine and *Ti-Pousse*. Those were the words Maybe-Gregory used in his poem. I try *Ti-Pousse* first, but there's nothing in this dictionary. I flip back to *K* and see *kine*. Archaic term for cows. Really? I try to remember where the poem was going. Wasn't he talking about balconies and D. W. Griffith? How did cows fit in with that? I guess you could make anything fit if you were good enough. I'm going to have to find that poem, but I don't think it's published yet.

I close the dictionary and scan the bookshelves again. I should know better than to look for a book of poems in Sophie's room. Besides the Paris book, there are just magazines. Most of them are gossip stories about stars like Marilyn Monroe, but there is a magazine that's all about Natalie Wood. I read that one cover to cover and then look through the pictures in the other magazines.

Solange is scratching at the door so I let her in. She jumps on my lap and curls up just like she did at home, which makes me feel better. I scratch her behind the ears until she has a really good purr going and lean back against the wall, looking at Sophie's stuff. There's a picture on Sophie's dresser of her mom doing a stand-up routine, and she looks just like Sophie.

I hear Nell-mom talking to Mrs. Tania while she gets a beer out of the fridge. I'm trying not to be angry at her, but the harder I try the angrier I get. I know in her mind she's doing the right thing, but I can't help feeling she could have tried harder to stay with Gary Daddy-o. And he could have tried harder, too. Maybe they should have fought more, like the couple I saw getting out of the Checker cab. Maybe then Gary Daddy-o would have listened to Nell-mom and they'd still be together. Then again, maybe not.

I look over at Sophie but she's put her glasses on the night table and her head is deep in the pillow so I know she's out cold. She never knew her father so I'm guessing she doesn't miss him. Of course, she might, but we never talk about it. When we were little, Gary Daddy-o used to give me piggyback rides around the apartment and if Sophie was there, he'd give her one, too. Maybe she wanted a daddy but just figured it would never happen.

I open the book about Paris because I'm starting to get angry again. They have cafés every other block it seems, restaurants, theaters, movies, and galleries. Sophie says she wants to move there when she turns eighteen and I might just go with her. I'd have to learn French but it looks like we're going to have to go to school anyway and I might as well learn something useful. Maybe we could go when we're fifteen, which is only three years from now. How old do you have to be before social workers leave you alone? Is Ray getting old enough to go on the road with Gary Daddy-o? If that happens, what will I do?

Solange curls her tail around her legs and hooks her paw over both of her eyes. If I do go to Paris, I'll have to figure out a way to take her with me. But for now it looks like I'm stuck here with school, Chaz, and sometime "visits" to Gary Daddy-o. Three years seems like a hundred, at least.

20
Real Beats

I WAKE UP shivering, with my face in the cushion and Solange asleep on my hair. I jump up and run to the bathroom, but there's no clock in there. Nell-mom and Mrs. Tania are asleep in the bedroom, and Chaz is long gone. I stand in the doorway, staring at Nell-mom. Her hair is spread out behind her, and her hand is under her cheek. I think of how she couldn't put her hands under the covers when she lived in a foster home and have to stop myself from getting teary. Part of me wants to walk over and lie down next to her, just to see if she'll open her eyes. I want to tell her I know she loves me, but she's making a big mistake breaking up with Gary Daddy-o. But if I do that, we'll just go around and around forever. We'll never get anywhere.

I tiptoe into the kitchen, where the floor is so cold it hurts my feet. There's a clock but I can't see it so

I open the refrigerator, hoping the light will help. Once the door's open I can see the time.

Ten thirty. I've got to get out of here.

I try waking Sophie but she's dead to the world. One of her sweaters is hanging over a chair and I pull it on, slip on shoes, and open the window. The street looks busy but it's pretty dark on the fire escape. I climb outside and pull the window down, leaving it open a little so I can get back inside. Sophie turns over in bed and pulls the covers around her, so I know she's still asleep.

I have to jump a few feet to get to the ground but luckily no one sees me. It's windier than it was when we got home so I button the sweater and start walking. There are people here and there on the sidewalk but it's not crowded; I'm thinking they're mostly inside somewhere. I've gone about two blocks when it starts to rain.

It's light rain at first, little drops glancing off my nose and forehead. I start walking faster and by the time I pass the leotard store on West Tenth the sky is opening up and it's starting to pour. I try pulling the sweater over my head but that doesn't work so I give up and start running. And then it really starts coming down, long needles of water as hard as nails. Lightning, too. I duck under an awning to think. Should I wait a few minutes? Go back? I don't want to, but I'm not really sure I should keep going. The guy who invited me—whoever he was—won't remember asking me. And I'm not really in the mood for poetry right now. I never thought I'd say that but it's true. So much happened and so much of it turned out bad. What difference would it make if I got to Chumley's anyway? I would still be losing Gary Daddy-o most of the time. I'd still be stuck with Chaz.

Suddenly the wind picks up and I'm getting pelted with rain, spitting ice-cold water at my ankles and into my shoes. There's no one on the street and I can't tell what time it is. I know it must be getting late, because most of the lights have gone off in the stores. How many minutes are left in my birthday? I don't want to spend those minutes here. But I don't want to go home, either. Birthdays are supposed to be adventures and this should have been one of the best.

I really wish Manuela was here. And then, thinking of her, I realize what she'd say. Don't let go of it, Ruby. Don't let go.

I pull my sweater up around my neck and start walking. By the time I reach Chumley's, I'm a sopping mess. *Bang!* I hit the door with the knocker as hard as I can but no one answers. *Bang!* I hit it again.

"Might have to call for them, kiddo."

I spin around to see Yogi, standing under an awning next door. He's totally dry and might as well be standing on a beach somewhere. I turn around again and call out, "Hey!"

Finally someone opens the panel on top of the door and says, "Yeah?" I can see an eye looking down at me.

"I'm here for the reading," I say.

"Yeah?"

"Gregory Corso invited me."

"Did he?"

"I think so," I say.

"Think so?" he repeats.

"Well, yeah—"

"Who is it?" a woman's voice calls.

A man in black jeans and a T-shirt opens the door. He's at least three shades better looking than anyone I've ever seen.

"When?" the man says.

"When what?"

"When did I invite you here?"

"Are you Gregory Corso?"

He squints at me, and I can tell he's starting to think I made the whole thing up. "Yeah, but I don't remember—"

"No," I say. "It wasn't you."

"Okay."

"But someone did," I say, "and I know that sounds dumb—"

"Hey, look at her," the woman says. "She's drenched."

Gregory opens the door wider, and the woman motions for me to come inside. I have a lot of questions but my teeth are chattering, so all I can manage is to nod my head at Yogi and say, "Can he come, too?"

"Yogi?" the woman asks, peering into the dark behind me.

"Hey." Yogi waves from underneath the awning. "I'm a little hungry—"

He shouldn't be, since guys who meditate aren't supposed to get hungry—or at least not so they admit it.

"Enter," the woman says, and Yogi follows me inside.

There's a big velvet curtain, and Gregory holds it open for us. As I get closer, I decide that whoever I met the night of Les and Bo's party must have thought I was an idiot. But if Gregory Corso is standing in front of me, who *was* that guy with the notebook?

"Honey," the woman says. "You wanna move?"

"Sorry," I say, and walk past Corso to the stairs. It's dark and hazy and smells like beer and ciga-rettes in here, but it feels really good to be out of the rain. We head upstairs and I try not to look over my shoulder at all the pictures of writers everywhere. When we get to the landing, the woman says that I'm freezing and need somebody's jacket. Someone passes a jacket to her and she hands it to me. It's black leather, lined with creases and grit.

"There you go," she says. My heart is pound-ing so hard I have to ball up my fists to keep from

shaking. I can't believe I'm here and Corso let me
in. Maybe that other guy's in here somewhere, too.
Who knows?

"I—thanks." I take off my sweater and put the
jacket on.

"How'd you find us?" the woman asks.

"Everybody knows where Chumley's is."

"Oh, yeah?" she says. "What's your name?"

"Ruby."

"Welcome, Ruby."

My heart is pounding even harder but I manage
to smile. "Thanks."

"Uh, guys?" Yogi calls out.

"I know," the woman says. She gets him a cup full of
pretzels and a glass of beer. He sits down in the corner.

"So, Ruby," the woman says, holding out her
hand to me. "I'm Diane."

"Hi." I pull my hand out of the jacket pocket and
she takes it.

"You okay?"

"Yeah."

"Your hand is ice-cold."

She introduces me to everyone: a guy they call
Charles with a face like sandpaper, a woman with
glasses named Elise, a man who goes by the initial T,
another guy named Peter, and someone else named
John. A few candles are burning, but it's pretty dark
in here and it takes me awhile to realize someone
else is in the room. But no one is talking to him.

He's lying on a couch in the back, and the couch is turned around so it's facing away from us. All I can see is a pair of long legs in blue jeans dangling off the end of the couch, and now and again, smoke from the end of a cigarette. I can't see his face, and his boots look old and worn. For some reason that gives me goose pimples. Could it be who I think it is?

I want to go over there, but if I do and I'm wrong, I'll feel really stupid. I jam my hands into the pockets of the jacket instead and look around the room. I'm thinking the reading should start but no one is saying much and all I hear is Yogi crunching pretzels. After a while I look at Diane.

"Am I too late? Did you finish already?"

Charles and Peter burst out laughing. "Are you kidding?" Diane says. "We haven't even started yet."

She pulls out a chair and asks if I want something.

"Um, coffee?" I've never had it but I think my choices are that and beer, and I'm not going to ask for water.

"Sure. You want cream and sugar?"

"Uh, no," I say. "I'll take it black."

Elise pours a cup and sets it down in front of me. I take a sip and put it down. No wonder people put cream and sugar in this stuff—it tastes like hot wax. I try to swallow without gritting my teeth so they at least think I've had it before.

"So, Ruby, you like readings?" Diane asks.

"I tried to get into The Scene a couple weeks ago—"

The guy on the couch stirs. For a few seconds, nobody says anything. Then Elise turns to me.

"You like to write?"

"Uh, sometimes."

"Did you bring something today?" Diane asks. Is she kidding? How could she be asking me to read for them? She must be having fun with me.

"Nah," I say. "I came here to listen to you guys."

"Leave her alone, Diane," says Charles, but Diane ignores him, smiling. "Well, if you ever feel . . . moved," she says. I'm pretty sure she's messing with me, but I'm not going to take the bait.

"That won't happen," I say. "But you guys go ahead."

And they do. Read, talk, argue, laugh, sing, and read again. Elise reads about loving someone who won't love you back, and Diane reads about a baby inside her and what the baby will find when it comes out. Charles reads three of his poems and they're all sad enough to make you cry.

After Charles, Gregory Corso reads a poem about marriage, which is really about not getting married, and that makes me think about Gary Daddy-o. Then he does one about laughing sickness and another about hitchhiking and I think, it's finally my birthday and isn't it funny? I'm here, where I wanted to be.

The man in the back puts his cigarette out, and I can see the top of his head. I know he's been listening to everyone but no one's talking to him and he doesn't say anything. He stretches his legs out and one of his boots falls onto the floor.

"So what do you think?" Elise asks, and I turn back to her.

"Well, yeah," I say. "I love it, I mean, it's . . . beautiful. Everything, I mean, all of it."

"No," Elise says. "I mean, what do you think about giving us one of your own?"

"Oh, no—not after listening to you guys."

"Oh, come on," says Diane. "We're all too drunk to know better anyway. We won't remember a thing you say."

They all start laughing and then I hear a voice coming from the back of the room. The man who's lying on the couch starts reciting, and not two words come out of his mouth when I feel like I want to die.

> *Sweet fleet beat of the street*
> *Rising heat*
> *From the white of the sidewalk*
> *And the conga sound of the*
> *Bonga bonga bongos*

"Please stop," I say. And he does.

I can tell they're all staring at me, but if I look up I think I'll run out or explode or something. I'm seeing Gary Daddy-o juggling his oranges, and of course I can't tell them that. So I just look down at my shoes, letting my hair fall over my eyes.

And then I hear the couch creaking, and I can tell the man who just spoke is getting up and either putting on his boots or kicking them off. Now he's walking over here. I want to look up but I can't. And then I do.

He squats in front of me, and I know right then.

He opens a notebook and hands it to me; I recognize it right away. I take the notebook without taking my eyes off his face—the face I wanted to see for years—and did see, except I didn't know it. He didn't want to tell me who he was the night I met him. I don't know why I thought he'd look like a statue or something, but he's the opposite—a regular guy with wrinkly jeans and hair on his forearms. It was him, sitting on the stoop beside me with the girl draped around him like a boa constrictor.

It was Kerouac.

He's in a blue shirt with rolled-up sleeves, and his hair is combed away from his forehead, which is long and broad. He's bigger than I thought but, at the same time, thinner, and I get the feeling he knows everything about me and everyone else here. But he knows how to wait and listen, too.

"You okay?" he says finally.

I nod.

He points to the poem I wrote in his notebook. "I like this."

I'm too embarrassed to talk about it, so I change the subject.

"Did you really write a book on toilet paper?"

For some reason that makes everyone laugh.

"It was *tracing* paper," he says. "Toilet paper was a rumor."

"Sorry," I say, and I can feel my face getting hotter by the second.

"No big deal." His eyes twinkle like we have a secret between us. But he doesn't say anything more and I realize he's not going to talk about his book or anything else he wrote. He wants me to give him something, but I don't know what it would be.

"Are you okay?" he asks again. The sound of his voice tells me he's really *asking*, not pretending to ask. I think he really does want to know.

"My mom is getting married," I say. "But not to my dad so I don't know if I'll see him much anymore." My mouth starts twitching and I put my hand over it so he won't see.

He nods like he wants me to keep talking, but I can't. After a minute he says, "Yeah," and then Corso nods, too, and I realize they're all with me. Everyone in this room had something happen to them, maybe not exactly like what happened to me, but similar. And in a way, that's why they're here.

I look down at the notebook again.

> *Every spring*
> *They sprout like toadstools*
> *In the key of heat*

I look up at Kerouac. "I don't know."

"What?"

"It's not what I want right now."

"What do you want?" he says. And I tell him.

> "Sad old song
> winding up inside my head.
> Alone like the song says,
> in a million songs,
> alone.
> I'm looking for something, I think you'd
> call it
> what I had.
> But I couldn't tell you what it was,
> just that I had it,
> like a penny or my shoes,
> bowl of cereal or a kiss.
> What I had
> and what I have, two different
> countries.
> But tonight there's only a sad old song
> singing over, over, over again."

I look down again and stop. I want to keep going but I can't. And, for a minute, it's really quiet. And then Kerouac says, "You have to write that, Ruby. You have to write that down."

"I think they're going to make me go to school," I say softly.

"It's okay," he says. "Write."

He hands me a pen and I scribble the words into the notebook. And when I look at him again, he's sitting on the floor in front of me.

"Do you feel better?"

"Sort of," I say, and he laughs.

"I had to go to reform school," Corso says. "But I ran away."

I turn to him. "Where'd you go?"

"Anywhere I could."

"I want to go to Paris."

"Yeah," he says. "Me, too."

Jack tears out the page with my poem and hands it to me. I fold it and put it in my pocket.

"Where else you want to go?" he asks.

"I don't know," I say. "I have a friend who's going to Mexico, but not because she wants to."

"Oh, yeah?"

"Her father went on strike at work so they're sending the family back to Mexico. That's where they're from."

"You want to write that, too," Jack says. I want to tell him about Manuela, about the hunger strike, about all the things I did after I met him. I want to tell him it's my birthday, I want to tell him a million things, but I know that's how everyone feels.

I hear snoring in the corner and look over at Yogi, who's fast asleep.

"S'all right," Charles says. "He sleeps here a lot of nights."

"I want to come back," I say. "Can I come back sometime?"

"We're here every weekend," Peter says. "Not all of us, but most."

I nod, watching Elise get up to read again. Just as she's about to start, she looks at me. "Don't worry, Ruby. I mean . . . you'll get to Paris, you know? I think we all get where we're going . . . eventually."

She starts reading, but this time it's one of Ginsberg's poems, calling out to his mother and saying farewell. It makes me think about saying that to Nell-mom and I decide I'm not ready. I'm mad at her but I still love her, even if she is driving me nuts right now.

I need to sit tight for a while, maybe meditate like Yogi so she'll get tired of Chaz and go back to Gary Daddy-o. In the meantime, I have to keep going over to his place and make sure he doesn't stay away from us. Keep his hopes up, and keep him and Ray coming home.

Right now, though, I'm sitting in a room full of the greatest poets in the world. I want to hear Kerouac read and I have a feeling he will before the night's over. It looks like I can come to Chumley's every once in a while and maybe write something really good one day if I ever get around to it. I don't think I'll ever be as good as these guys, but you never know.

Like Elise says, we all get where we're going eventually. So maybe the stuff you go through when

you're a kid, no matter how rotten, is what spurs you
to get wherever you want to be. The main thing is
not to give in to what everyone else wants and keep
doing what you do best. Because, when all is said
and done, you know—that's all you mostly have.
That's what Beats know. What it means in here and
on all the Beat streets.

> *Every spring*
> *In the key of heat*
> *Sweet, fleet Beat Street*

That's what it means.

Reader's Guide

When I started work on *The Beat on Ruby's Street*, I was looking for kids. Were there any in Greenwich Village in the 1950s? Were their parents artists? Some of the Beat poets had children, but they didn't talk about them much, and not much has been written about their lives. After a while, I gave up trying to find a real kid and created one of my own. I'd always wanted to grow up in a place saturated with art and artists, so I folded the childhood I wished for into a story. And, as stories do, it slipped away and turned into *The Beat on Ruby's Street*.

I can tell you a lot about the Beat generation, but so much has been written I think it best to give you a quick sampler and link you up to websites that will help you find more. One of my favorite stories, and the one I started with, is about Jack Kerouac's novel *On the Road* being written on a long, continuous roll of paper.

You may think Beats started writing poetry in the 1950s, but things really got rolling in the 1940s in New York and San Francisco. Jack Kerouac supposedly coined the term "Beats," which meant beaten down by society with no prospects for success. Poets like Allen Ginsberg, Lawrence Ferlinghetti, and Gregory Corso were part of the scene and became known for questioning authority and mainstream America.

Allen Ginsberg's first book *Howl and Other Poems* is thought to have spurred the first wave of the Beat generation's poetry. *Howl* was published by Lawrence Ferlinghetti's press City Lights; and Ferlinghetti was brought to trial the next year on obscenity charges. The judge ruled the poem was not obscene and the case brought enormous attention to Ginsberg and other Beat poets.

Though the most famous Beat artists are Jack Kerouac, Allen Ginsberg, Gregory Corso and William Burroughs, there are tons of Beat writers whose work is exceptional, including women who played a significant role in the inspiration for this book. Elise Cowen, Diane di Prima, Hettie Jones, Denise Levertov, and Anne Waldman wrote superbly during the years when Beat poetry was flourishing—and there were many more.

Movies like *Howl, On the Road*, and *Kill Your Darlings* can show you how Beat writers are portrayed by Hollywood, but the only real way to find out what they cared about is to read their work. I hope you'll check out some of my favorites:

"Constantly Risking Absurdity" — Lawrence Ferlinghetti
"My Alba" — Allen Ginsberg
"Weather" — Hettie Jones
"Trees" — Jack Kerouac
"People at Night" — Denise Levertov

To learn more, read *This Is the Beat Generation* by John Clellon Holmes from the *New York Times*, *The Beat Book* (edited by Anne Waldman), and *The Portable Beat Reader* by Ann Charters.

Questions for Discussion

1. Given Ruby's patchy eating habits, do you think she was trying to take the orange from the fruit stand? Or was she falsely accused?

2. What kinds of subjects do you think Ruby and her friends cover at Blue Skies? What would you choose to study if you were with them?

3. Ruby believes poetry (and art) aren't good for anything except "making you feel better." Do you agree? Why or why not?

4. Things seem a lot easier for Ray than for his sister, Ruby. Is it because of Ray's personality, or how people treat him? Do you think there are other reasons things seem to go better for Ray?

5. There's a saying that "the road to hell is paved with good intentions." What choices could the

characters have made so things might have turned out differently?

6. Does Ruby's relationship with Manuela change her life? What does Manuela learn from Ruby?

7. Is Ruby's mother making the right decision in order to bring Ruby home?

8. What role does Ruby's cat, Solange, play in the book?

9. Sophie's mother is a comedy writer, which was extremely rare for women in 1958. Can you find any examples of other nontraditional roles played by women in the 1950s?

10. What do you think Ruby learns about herself at the end of the book?

A Sneak Peek at

FOOL'S ERRAND: Book 2

1—UNDER A BRIDGE

SOPHIE IS missing.

I don't know for how long, but I know she's gone.

She's my best friend in the world, since forever. Not exactly a Beat Generation-artist-type 'cause her mother was rich, but Mrs. T was the best comedy writer in town and the best mom to Sophie. (Sometimes I wish she was my mom).

If you want to help me look, Sophie's mother's name is Annie Tanya. I call her Mrs. T sometimes because it's quicker, and she doesn't seem to mind.

I say she *was* rich because the pile of money Mrs. T made is shrinking, and that happened because she lost her job. Something about the Blacklist, which is connected to how the government sees you, but it's dumb because Mrs. Tanya doesn't care about politics.

Funny isn't easy, she always says, but she makes it look that way. She's written scripts for a ton of TV shows and is mainly the only lady comedy writer in the world. She worked with guys like Mel Brooks, Carl Reiner, and Neil Simon—some of the funniest funny men in the world—and a few years back wrote for Your Show of Shows with Sid Caesar and

Imogene Coca. That was 1954, just four years ago, and she worked there just about four years, too. A producer named Max brought her into the business. I know every big shot in town is named Max, but that really is his name.

Sophie's mom is also beautiful, like a dark-haired Doris Day, and I always thought she could be a great actress. But Sophie's the real actress in the family. And since both of us were little, Mrs. T tried out her jokes on us and made us laugh.

Here's what I learned works best when you're trying to be funny:

- Bad jokes work best in the middle of an argument
- Hiccups can be funny, but not as funny as you think
- Jokes about politicians and people and things we know
- Things we think and never say
- Saying them in funny voices (Sophie's specialty)

No one knows if Mrs. T is going to get the chance to be funny anymore because of the Blacklist—which isn't something you can find lying around, but it exists the same as we do. You only mostly get on the list if someone at the House UnAmerican Activities Committee (HUAC) in Congress accuses you of being a Communist. I asked Sophie what that meant, and she says Communists are people in Russia who rebelled against rich guys who were lording it over everyone else.

But then somehow or other, this maniac named Josef Stalin took over, and he started killing everyone right and left, and even though he's dead, the people who took over are still dictators.

Mainly I think Congress believes everyone in Russia has cooties, which is what the kids around here say about people nobody likes. And Congress doesn't want Americans to get them.

A lot of writers and actors in Hollywood thought the Communists were good guys at first, and then those writers and actors changed their minds. But that House committee thinks there's still a lot of Communists running around over here, and have to be "rooted out."

The HUAC folks started pulling all these actors in to court hearings and asking them questions. "Did you ever go to a meeting with Communists? Who are the Communists you know?" Mrs. T's husband brought her to some meetings a long time ago, but she was never a Communist. She just went to the meetings because he asked her to go.

But if the committee wants you to name the people you met at meetings, they want you to rat on your friends, who are just like Mrs. T and didn't mean any harm. If the committee asks you questions and you don't want to answer them, you can say "I plead the Fifth," which means you don't have to speak about anything that could hurt you in court.

Except... once you plead the Fifth, the committee sends your name to all the producers in Hollywood and New York and you get blacklisted, and no one, I mean NO one, will hire you anymore. Period.

Plus some people even go to jail if they don't name their friends.

This whole Blacklist thing didn't just happen to Mrs. T—it happened to a lot of people, and because Sophie and her mom are Jewish, somehow that makes it worse, because a lot of people say bad things about Jews, which is stupid. Mrs. T's producer Max is Jewish too, and he's also in trouble with the House committee.

What happened was Mrs. T wrote a sketch for a play that a group of actors were doing. Some were on the Blacklist already, and they wanted to let audiences know what was happening. The sketch Mrs. T wrote was pretty funny and made it look like all you had to do was eat red cereal to be called a Communist.

Except somebody who saw the play told the House Committee that Mrs. T *was* a Communist. And because Max helped produce the play, he got in trouble too, and both Max and Mrs. T got fired. That wasn't fair *at all*, because it's a free country and you're supposed to be able to write whatever you want. Except Congress doesn't see it that way.

The weird thing is, nobody thought this stuff

could even happen in 1958. The Blacklist has been going on for like ten, twelve years, but it's still happening and no one knows when it will end, if ever.

I don't know how it started exactly, but there was a senator named Joseph McCarthy going after Communists in the government until he died a few years ago. Then the House of Representatives started bothering entertainers. If you don't answer them the way they want, they write your name on a list that says you're "Red," which is the same thing as Communist. They share it with the papers and everyone else.

My mother Nell—I call her Nell-mom—says the suits in Congress just want you to *conform*, which means going to work and wearing ties, and if you're a woman, staying home making Jell-O.

I hate Jell-O.

In Greenwich Village, here, Beats try to do the opposite of conforming, because we want to do things differently from regular people. And the last thing anyone expected was for Mrs. T and her producer Max to get this House committee on their tails.

For as long as I've known them, Sophie and her mom were going gangbusters through the world. They had the biggest apartment I'd ever seen, and I loved going over there.

When Mrs. T lost her job in May, she tried to find some way to write on the Q-T, which means the down-low. You have to make up a name, or just write something and let someone else take the credit. I would hate that, but Mrs. T says she'd be lucky to find that kind of thing.

But because most of the writers are cats—I mean guys, not chicks—I mean ladies—it's harder for Mrs. T to find work. She has some money saved up, but she also has to pay a lawyer in case those Congress guys bring her in for questioning. And lawyers are *expensive*, which means they cost a *lot*.

When Mrs. T had to stop working at the TV station, she started having trouble paying rent, because the apartment she and Sophie live in is expensive, too. And since Sophie's dad left the family years ago, Mrs. T has to come up with every penny.

Nell-mom said they could crash at our place for a while—I've got bunk beds and there's a fold-out in the living room—and they were here for a couple of weeks. Mrs. T told my mom they couldn't impose on us any more, even though Nell-mom said we were in no hurry to get rid of them, which I didn't like because it sounded like they were pets. But Mrs. Tanya said she thought they should go to New Jersey, where they have relatives. Except Sophie told me later that's a story like the ones her mom makes up for TV.

Now it's June and school's out, which is good, because Sophie and me and our friend Gordy were really looking forward to being free for the summer. This year was the first time any of us had ever been to a real school, because we were mostly learning on our own at a store called Blue Skies in the neighborhood. The owners picked that name because their names are Sky and Blu.

Like I said, Beats don't usually do what everyone else does, unless a social worker makes us. Which is what happened this year—and it's why we had to start going to a regular school. Today was our last day, and Gordy wanted to get sodas at Rocco's to celebrate, even though we'd only been in classrooms for a month and half. I think I can speak for everyone and say that was more school than any Beat should put up with, and we don't want to go back in the fall.

Sophie said she'd see us later, 'cause she wanted to go home and see her mom. That was the last I saw of her, walking down Bleecker and heading over to Charles, getting smaller and smaller as she walked away.

I would have been home sooner, but it started raining buckets all of a sudden, and Gordy and I stayed inside Rocco's a while, waiting for it to stop. It didn't stop exactly, but there was a break in the rain and we both left and by the time I got home, all the suitcases were gone and there was no Sophie and no Mrs. T.

That was around five, and now it's close to midnight and extremely hot and humid, so you feel like you're in a bathtub when you go outside, or even stick your head out the window like Mrs. Belusa does at my old digs on Perry Street when she's yelling at you. We saw that Mrs. T left a note about that New Jersey relative, but of course I know better. I tried to tell Nell-mom, but she refuses to get upset.

I think Nell-mom changed after she married Chaz. She thinks it's a good change, but I'd argue differently. She's worried about me and my older brother Ray getting mad at her, so she's always trying to be as sweet as pie, which feels like she turned into the kind of mom you'd see on TV—not that we have a television.

Because Chaz owns a gallery and charges high prices for his paintings (including Nell-mom's), we get to live in a nice pad and things are mostly comfy-cozy. That's if you don't mind having your real dad on the road all the time and your brother skipping out whenever he can to join your father's band.

Nell-mom has this thing, and she says all mothers have it: they want their kids to be happy. She'd do anything to make me happy, she says, and I don't think I can tell her this, but if you try too hard, sometimes you do the opposite. Nell-mom is definitely, truly, completely trying too hard.

When I try to get her riled up over something, and I used to be pretty good at it, she smiles and acts real patient and wants to talk through what's bothering me.

That's nasty. And I even think she knows it.

"There's no New Jersey relatives," I tell her. "Sophie and her mom are under a bridge somewhere."

"Oh, Ruby," she says. "Annie must have had a good reason for leaving, and she would have told me if she and her daughter had nowhere to go. She wouldn't put Sophie at risk like that."

"How do you know?" I ask.

Nell-mom frowns. "What do you want me to do?"

I look at her, trying to figure out how far she'll let me go.

"Come out with me and look for them?"

"It's nearly midnight. You need to go to bed," Nell-mom replies.

"How can I?"

"We'll look tomorrow, Ruby."

"Tomorrow could be too late."

"I'm sure Annie knows what she's doing," Nell-mom says. "I trust her."

I shake my head and look out the window, while Nell-mom goes over to the kitchen table and picks up a sketch pad to draw. I'm thinking about this couple I saw once under the Brooklyn Bridge when we had a school field trip about a month ago. A man and a woman sharing a sandwich, and when you got closer, you could see their clothes were dirty and torn, and the woman's eyes were hungry, like an alley cat's outside a diner at closing time.

How did that couple land under that bridge? Where did they live before? Did they have a wedding with a white dress and cake like Nell-Mom and Chaz? Or did they just sort of live together like Nell-mom and my father Gary Daddy-o? Do they have kids? And if they do, are the kids in a children's home like I was for a while, until Nell-mom said she'd get married and brought me home? Did the man lose his job? Did either one of them even have jobs?

And why isn't Nell-mom worried? Maybe it's because she worries so much about me and Ray she doesn't have room to worry about anyone else. Or maybe she just wants to focus on her art now that she finally has a little more money than she used to. Whatever the problem is, I don't think I can get her upset about it. She's just too focused on staying calm.

I put my hands on the kitchen window, which is starting to fog up with drizzle. *Sophie, please don't be under the Brooklyn Bridge tonight.* I close my eyes and all I can do is think of you with your mom, trying to eat a roll you found in the garbage somewhere. What if you don't even find that much?

I'm happy it's not cold, but I'm also worried about where you'll be when it turns cold. Luckily that won't happen for a while. June is the month when the sun gets hotter and brighter, bongos are everywhere like sprouts all over the streets, and fruit blossoms into bunches of green, red, orange and yellow on the bins outside stores. So it's a pretty nice time to be outside.

That doesn't mean I want to hightail it out of here right this minute. But I can't sit around here worrying. I just can't.

Ray's in his room, getting ready to meet Gary Daddy-o tomorrow on a gig in Maryland. He stuck around for the rest of the school year, but I have a feeling he'll be gone until next fall. He understands about Sophie and her mom though, and even offered them his room for the summer. I just think Mrs. T was too proud to take it.

I wonder if Ray would go out with me, since Nell-mom looks tired, and once she and Chaz go to bed, we hardly see them until morning. I look out the window again, watching the soft white shine of streetlights on the building next door.

I start remembering all the slumber parties Sophie and I had growing up. Nights like this, we'd tell ghost stories with a flashlight until we both cracked up. We talked about moving to Paris when we both turn 16, which is four years away since we both turned twelve this year. My birthday was in April and Sophie's was in February.

Whenever we talked about leaving, we said we'd wait tables at a café and get clothes that would be *trés chic* so we could go to theater parties. Of course we'd have to learn French so I could write poetry like I want to do, and she could act in plays and TV shows.

She must have known they were leaving.

I knock on Ray's door and he says, "Come in."

He'll be 16 in September, and is starting to get tall and lean like Gary Daddy-o even though he looks mostly like Nell-mom, with blue eyes and curly hair. He's got his suitcase open on the bed and the whole room's a mess, with shirts and jeans and jackets strewn everywhere. Even the pictures on the walls have undershirts hanging from their corners. I ask him to go out and look for Sophie and her mom with me.

"Where?" he asks, and I stare at him. "Where do we even look?"

Good question. I look outside, trying to imagine where I'd go if I was Sophie.

"We could start with restaurants and stuff in the neighborhood—"

"They're not in a restaurant," Ray says.

"Where, then?"

"I don't know," he says. "They went somewhere far, don't you think? Train station? They'd buy their tickets and wait around for their train? I don't think they'd ride the rails."

No, that wouldn't be Mrs. Tanya's style, though the idea of it makes me think of Sophie in a comedy movie, wearing an oversized hat and floppy coat.

"Where would they get a train?" I ask. "Where would they go?"

"I don't know," Ray replies. "But they'd buy their

tickets at Grand Central Station on Forty-Second Street."

"Can we go there?"

"I'll go, but we're taking a taxi," says Ray. "I'm not waiting for a bus right now."

All of a sudden, I'm loving my Ray-Ray because ever since Gary Daddy-o and Nell-mom split up, he's become the kind of brother I always wanted him to be. Whatever he gets from his gigs with Gary Daddy-o, he spends, and it's usually on other people—which is just about the most Beat thing you can possibly do. Even if part of him knows this may well be a fool's errand that won't work out, Ray won't complain. He'll just dummy up and ride along.

You probably know this already, but Beats don't like money or buying too much stuff—or much of anything else that makes most people happy. Poets like Jack Kerouac say the Beats are "the root, the soul of Beatific," "rising from underground, the "hipsters of America." That's how Ray and I were raised to be. Just don't call us Beatniks—that's a Hollywood word.

"Think we'll find a taxi?" I ask.

"No idea," Ray says, closing the apartment door as quietly as he can.

"Let's go down a few blocks to the avenue?" I ask, and he frowns, but walks along with me. Luckily, a cab stops when we've only gone a little ways and a lady gets out. We rush inside before the cabbie can turn around.

"What the—"

"Grand Central," I tell him. "And step on it."

I've just always wanted to say that.

But the cabbie gives me more than I bargained for. He's weaving in and out of streets and nearly runs into three other cabs trying to get us there. I don't even know what streets we're on because he's going so fast. All I can do is cringe when I hear his brakes squealing, which happens every other second. When he finally pulls up to the curb at Grand Central Station, I'm practically drenched from sweating buckets, but Ray is laughing hysterically. He pays the cabbie and I jump out, fighting the urge to kiss the ground.

"Keep the change," Ray says, and I grab his hand and pull him towards me. I don't want either one of us near that cab again for the rest of our lives. Ray lets me drag him into Grand Central before he drops my hand.

"Where—"

"This way," Ray says, pointing towards the central ticket booths.

"No," I tell him. "If they're here, they'll be in the waiting room."

We walk through the station, edging closer to the benches. It looks like there are mostly single people waiting for their trains, but here and there you can spot families, with kids wailing or trying to go to sleep. A guy is feeding dog biscuits to a German shepherd and someone else is cooing to what seems like a guinea pig in a cage. For some reason, it's not noisy even though a ton of people are here. In fact, it's not noisy at all.

Sophie, Sophie, where are you?

"Look, Ruby!"

Ray's voice shatters the quiet and I stop in my tracks to look at him. Wouldn't you know it, he's pointing upward at the ceiling.

"What are you—"

"Just look!"

Twinkly yellow stars and constellations in a turquoise sea meet my eyes.

"Zodiac," Ray says, and for once I don't want to tease him about being obvious, because I never learned much about stars at Blue Skies. I was hectoring Sky and Blu to take me to the Planetarium, but they never got around to it. This zodiac mural has a lot of cool stuff, like Aquarius, the water carrier; Pisces, the fish; Aries, the ram; Taurus, the bull; Gemini, the twins; and Cancer, the crab; plus constellations like Orion, the hunter.

Normally I'd stand here staring at this stuff for hours, but I'm just too worried right now. "It's great, Ray," I tell him, "but we've got to find Sophie."

"Just for a second, Ruby," says Ray. "See Pegasus?"

I've read about Pegasus in a comic they had at Blue Skies. I think he was Sophie's favorite, because she loves horses and this one could fly. I can't help but think of her looking up at him tonight.

"Just wanted you to see," Ray says, and then for some reason, or no reason at all, my eye falls on a bench with a mother and daughter at the opposite end of the station room. Maybe it was Pegasus; maybe it was just taking my eye off the benches for a while; or maybe it was just the color blue they used on the zodiac that perked me up, but I felt like I could see more clearly now than I had since Sophie disappeared.

The woman had dark chin-length hair like Mrs. T and her daughter's was only a teeny bit longer—like Sophie's. I couldn't tell if the girl had glasses, but it looked like she had a royal-blue sweatshirt the exact same color as my friend's, and the back of her head—leaning on her mother's shoulder—was exactly the same.

I ran like the wind, faster than Pegasus, with Ray right behind and then overtaking me. He practically flew at the bench, blocking my view until I grabbed at his shirt and he stopped, suddenly, his sneakers squeaking on the marble tiles of the floor.

"Soph?" I call, but when the woman looks up at me all I see are the tired eyes of a stranger. I can tell Ray is staring at me but I don't want to look at him. If I do, I'll have to admit something, and I don't want to own it right now. Both of us know it anyway.

Sophie's gone.

About the Author

Jenna Zark is a columnist, lyricist, playwright, and novelist. Her play *A Body of Water* was published by Dramatists Play Service and produced regionally after its debut at Circle Repertory in New York. Other plays were produced in the Twin Cities, Los Angeles, Atlanta, and St. Louis. As a former staff writer at *Scholastic Choices* magazine, Zark wrote extensively for middle school and junior high students on a range of topics. Zark's columns, poetry, essays, and articles have been published in the online magazine *TC Jewfolk*, *Stoneboat* literary magazine, the Jewish daily newspaper *The Forward*, and numerous other publications. Zark is also a member of a composer-lyricist group in the Twin Cities. She's still trying to figure out if it's harder to write a play, a novel, or a song. To share your thoughts on that or to learn more, please visit *jennazark.com*.

CPSIA information can be obtained
at www.ICGtesting.com
Printed in the USA
LVHW111719120819
627348LV00001B/34/P

Clara Caterpillar

Clara Caterpillar

by Pamela Duncan Edwards • illustrated by Henry Cole

SCHOLASTIC INC.

New York   Toronto   London   Auckland   Sydney
Mexico City   New Delhi   Hong Kong   Buenos Aires

One day a cream-colored butterfly laid an egg
on a cabbage leaf.

"Grow up to be courageous and contented, Clara,"
she called to her egg as the wind carried her away.

Clara lay curled in the egg case for a considerable time. Eventually a crowd of caterpillars clustered around her.

"She's incredibly late coming out," commented one.

"She's very cautious," agreed another.

A curious caterpillar knocked
on Clara's egg case.
"This is Cornelius," he said.
"Come on out!"
"But I'm comfortable
in here," called Clara.

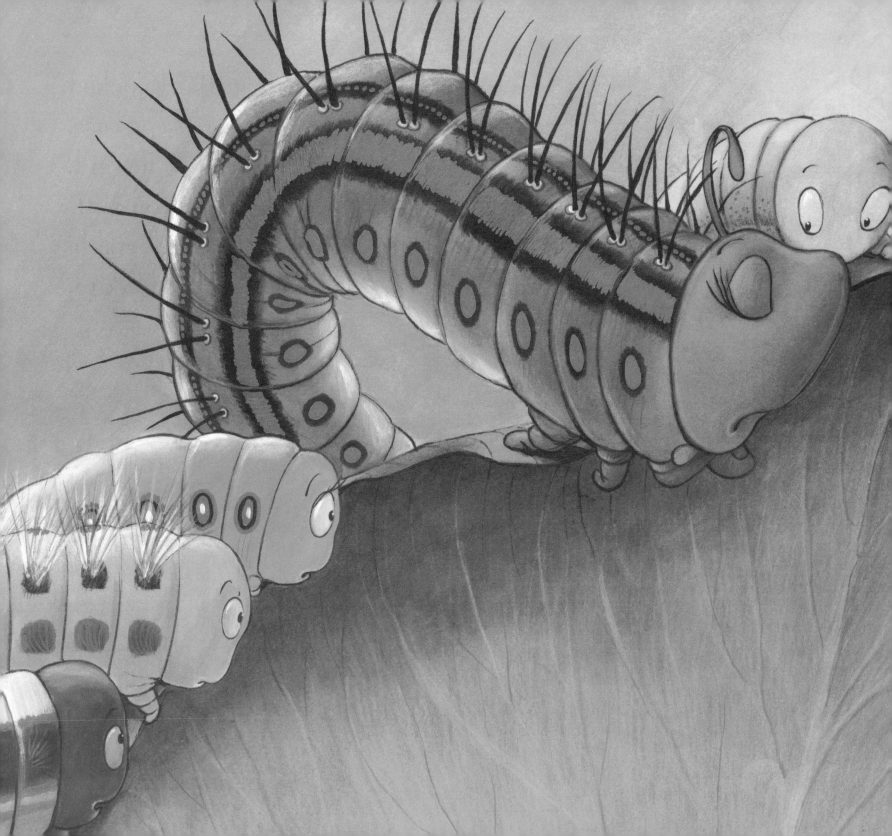

"Who cares if she comes out?" scoffed a scowling caterpillar called Catisha. "It's clear she'll only be a cabbage caterpillar. Cabbage caterpillars are so common."

"Don't be cruel, Catisha," Cornelius scolded. "Cabbage caterpillars are cute."

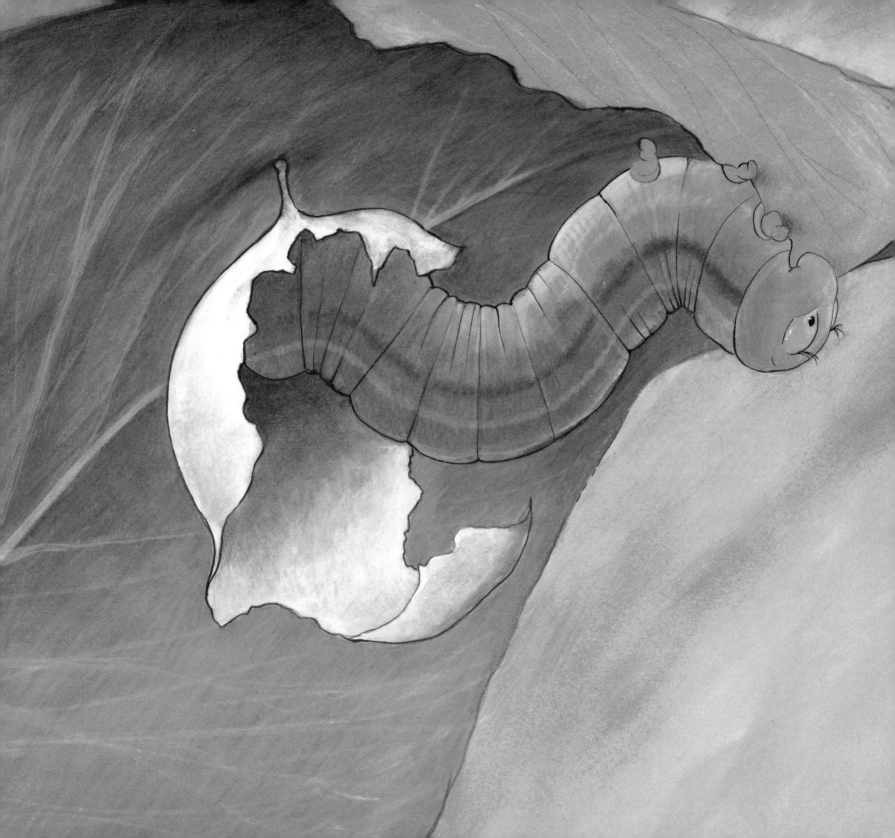

"Did you say cabbage?" cried Clara. "Cabbage sounds scrumptious!" So Clara cut a hole in her egg case and clambered out.

"I'm a lucky caterpillar," she said. "Cornelius! Come and share this delectable cabbage!"

Clara and Cornelius climbed and crawled and capered about. They had carefree caterpillar fun.

They crammed themselves with cabbage, carrot, and cauliflower leaves.

They grew into colossal caterpillars.

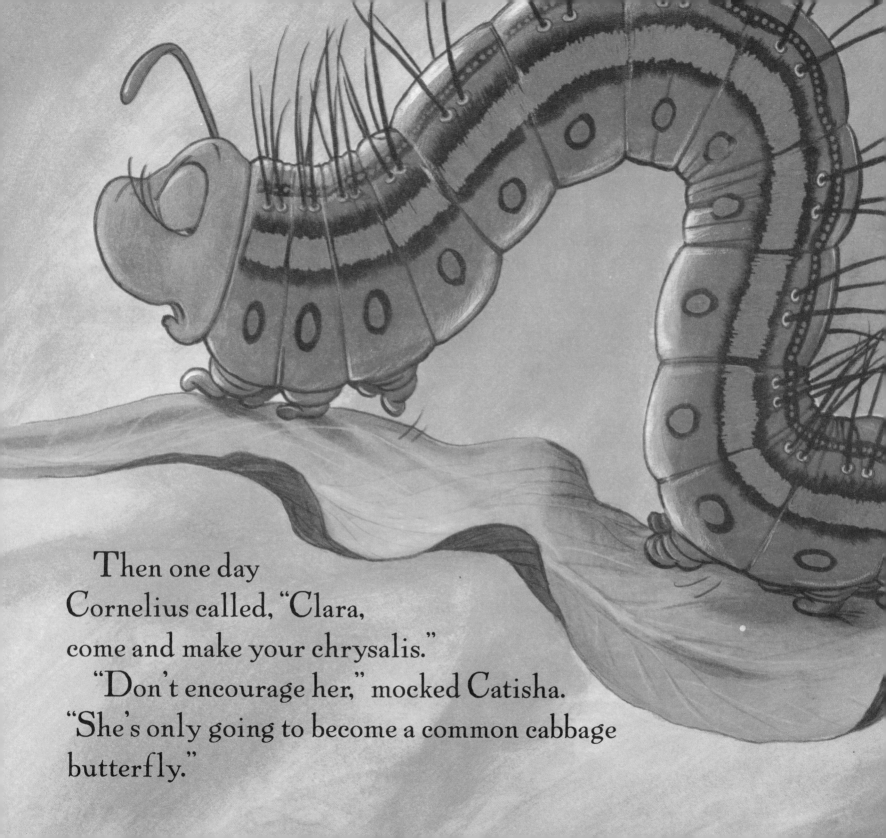

Then one day
Cornelius called, "Clara,
come and make your chrysalis."
"Don't encourage her," mocked Catisha.
"She's only going to become a common cabbage
butterfly."

"Why is Catisha
being catty?" Clara asked.
"Catisha is conceited," comforted Cornelius.
"She knows she'll become an attractive
crimson-colored butterfly."

Then Clara, Cornelius, and the other
caterpillars caught on to the cabbage,
carrot, and cauliflower plants
with cottony threads.

They crinkled and discarded their skins
and cuddled down inside their chrysalises.

"I'm crushed in here."

"I'm creased!"

"I'm crumpled!"

"I hate being cooped up."

"I'm cramped!"

"I'm coiled like a corkscrew."

"My back tickles!"

"I can't scratch!"

"It's making me CRANKY!"

"I can't cope!" complained Catisha.

"Coo-ey!" cried Cornelius to Clara. "Are you comfortable?"

"Actually, I'm very cozy," Clara called back.

Then, one morning, the chrysalises began to crack, and out climbed delicate creatures.

"Coooool!" cried Clara. "You all look captivating! Cornelius, you're a terrific copper color!"

"Why is that scruffy creature conversing with us?" complained a scowling crimson-colored butterfly.

"Catisha!" Clara said. "You are SPECTACULAR!"

"Of course," replied Catisha.
"And you, Clara, are so CREAM!"
"I think cream is cute," declared Cornelius.
"Cute!" Catisha snickered. "Don't be ridiculous, Cornelius!"

Then Catisha climbed toward the clouds on her scaly cobweb wings.

Suddenly a crow cawed and scared everyone. "Snacktime!" he exclaimed as he caught sight of the crimson-colored Catisha. The butterflies panicked and frantically scattered in all directions.

"You can't escape!" screeched the crow to Catisha.
"Catisha! I'm coming to the rescue!" cried Clara.
"Clara, be careful," screamed Cornelius.
Plucking up her courage, Clara flicked
her wings at the crow.

"Catch me if you can, you scalawag!"
she taunted.

Then Clara curved down and ducked
into a camellia bush.

The crow became confused and forgot about Catisha. He cocked his head and pecked in the petals. But Clara, the cream-colored butterfly, lay camouflaged behind a curtain of cream-colored camellias.

"That's curious," complained the crestfallen crow. "I was confident I could capture a succulent snack."

"The coast is clear!" Cornelius shouted.
"The crisis is over!"

"Congratulations, Clara," complimented
the other butterflies.

"Clara, you're so clever," cried the shocked
Catisha. "I could never camouflage myself like you.
I'm too colorful. I was crazy to scoff at your cream
color. It's incredible."

"And cute, too!" declared Cornelius.

Cornelius clapped his wings.
"Listen carefully," he commanded. "That crow is
a scoundrel! Let's cling close to Clara. Clara can stop
him from catching us. Clara is so capable and courageous."
"Clara is lucky to be cream colored," said Catisha.

"And I'm a completely contented butterfly," said Clara.

To sweet Alex—
may you grow up to be
courageous and contented

—P.D.E.

For Marion, whose appreciation
and respect for nature
has always been an inspiration to me

—H.C.

ISBN 0-439-40016-3

Text copyright © 2001 by Pamela Duncan Edwards. Illustrations copyright © 2001 by Henry Cole.
All rights reserved. Published by Scholastic Inc., 557 Broadway, New York, NY 10012,
by arrangement with HarperCollins Publishers. SCHOLASTIC and associated logos
are trademarks and/or registered trademarks of Scholastic Inc.

12 11 10 9   3 4 5 6 7/0

Printed in the U.S.A.   08

First Scholastic printing, May 2002

Typography by Elynn Cohen